KING FORTIS

The Brave!

ISBN 1-59113-068-9

Published 2002

Published by Booklocker, P.O. Box 2399, Bangor, ME 04402, USA.

Manufactured in the United States of America.

Cover Art by Ken Wilson
Cover design by Paul Cammilleri

Booklocker.com, Inc.
2002

KING FORTIS

The Brave!

MICHAEL R. LaMONTAGNE
AND RONALD E. SNYDER

For Kim, Remi and Anika

For Sherene, Therese, Jenna, Gabrielle and Erin

With love

CONTENTS

PROLOGUE

"Who dares?"

Galen flinched as he entered the foul chamber, pausing to let his eyes adjust to the darkness. A pitiful form came into focus, and he had to force himself to look away from the figure writhing in pain. He directed his attention instead toward the tall woman standing alongside the torture rack. "Please forgive the intrusion, mistress Haeron, but you wanted to be notified as soon as Natrix returned."

Haeron gave the wheel a final twist. "Bring the prophet to me at once", she commanded, shouting to be heard over the screams of her victim.

"As you wish."

The man being tortured on the rack was guilty of one crime only. He had kept Haeron waiting. Galen saw to it that Natrix was whisked to the dungeon immediately. The guards leading the prophet bowed their heads in the presence of their queen, but Natrix held her own head high as she walked into the chamber. "I have finished," she said simply.

"You have located Archimagus for me?" Haeron asked.

"No. The stars tell me only what will be, not what already is."

"Then tell me what will be," Haeron snapped. "And be quick about it, if you value your life."

"The stars have told me a great deal about Archimagus," Natrix answered with a deliberate, spiteful sluggishness. "The magician will soon come out of his centuries of hiding to herald in the second coming of King Fortis, and together they will liberate Daak from its greatest enemy. You."

Haeron's pale face turned a deep shade of red and she had to fight to maintain her composure. "I hired you to locate the one magician on the entire planet that has eluded my grasp and all I get from you is a millennium-old Truculan myth."

"The legend of Fortis is no myth, and his return will come to pass sooner than you think. Beware. Even as we speak Archimagus is preparing for his return. And if events continue to progress as they are, you will be dethroned and Daak given back to her people during the feast of midsummer."

Haeron thought this over. She didn't want to believe what she was hearing, but the prophecies of Natrix were never wrong. "Is there anything I can do to prevent this from coming about?"

"Not so long as Archimagus remains free, but there is one way to beat prophesy. Capture the magician. Enslave him. Or better yet, put him to death. With Archimagus neutralized before the feast of midsummer, prophesy cannot be fulfilled and your reign of terror will know no end."

"Excellent. You have done well, prophet."

Natrix nodded her head. "We had an agreement, Haeron, and I have upheld my end of the bargain. I expect to be paid in full."

"Don't worry," Haeron said as she gently stroked the now lifeless body on her torture rack. "You will get exactly what is coming to you."

CHAPTER ONE
The Apple

Rodney was bored. He sat at his bedroom window watching the last few patches from yesterday's snowfall melt in the sun. A thought crossed his mind, a thought that frightened him. He missed school. No, he quickly reminded himself. It wasn't school that he missed, it was just one class. Art. It was the only class that interested him, and the only one he received good grades from. The rest of the school could burn down for all he cared as long as the art room remained intact.

He slipped away from the window and sat down at the drawing table that his parents had given him for Christmas last year. If he couldn't work on his art project at school, at least he could do something at home. With renewed energy he grabbed some paper and his colored pencils and went to work. Before long he had transformed a blank piece of paper into a beautiful country scene. A blue sparkling brook snaked its way between grass-covered hills while a small village nestled peacefully in the background. Rodney was pleased with what he was creating, and so caught up in his work that he almost didn't hear his bedroom door open.

"Happy Thanksgiving," a girl's voice said. It was his twin sister Aimee.

"Go away."

"I don't have to. This is my house too, you know."

"Maybe so," Rodney admitted, "but this is my room, so go away."

"I'm not leaving until you agree to come out and play with me. The sun's out and it's almost fifty degrees. Mom says that this might be the last warm day we have before winter sets in."

"Fifty degrees isn't warm," Rodney answered. He was in one of those moods where he was going to argue no matter what his sister said.

"It is for this time of year, now come on. Let's go play. We still have about three hours before Thanksgiving dinner."

Dinner. Now there was a word that caught Rodney's attention. And not just any dinner, but Thanksgiving dinner! His mouth watered at the thought of turkey and stuffing with lots of gravy. There would also be mashed potatoes, yams, applesauce, cranberry sauce and best of all, to top it all off, a slice of the banana cream pie that his father made every year. Just the thought of all that food lifted Rodney's spirits. Especially the pie. There wasn't anything in the world he liked better than his father's banana cream pie. Of course he would go out to play, if for no other reason than to work up a big appetite so he could eat more at dinner.

* * *

As the screen door to the back porch swung shut behind them, Rodney made a dash toward the swing set. "Last one there loves Donnie Lardin," he shouted, knowing full well that with the head start he had gotten his sister could never catch up with him.

"No fair," Aimee protested as she deliberately slowed her pace. When she got to the swings Rodney was already standing on top of the slide acting like he was king of the backyard. Aimee sat down on the higher of the two swings and looked up at him. "It's boring back here. Let's do something different."

"Like what?"

Aimee kicked her legs and set a swing in motion. "I dunno, but I don't want to stay here. You pick something to do."

Rodney thought a moment. "What we need is an adventure. Maybe we can explore the woods behind the school."

Before his sister could respond, he shot his own idea down. "Nah, I've done that hundreds of times. Besides, with all the melting snow it's got to be too muddy back there. Forget the woods. I know where we can go. Come on."

Rodney ran down the slide, his steps echoing loudly as his feet clanged against the plastic chute. He stumbled a little as he landed on the ground but was able to maintain his balance and continue running, straight out the gate that led to the sidewalk. Aimee jumped off the swing and chased him down the street and around the corner.

"Wait up," she shouted, panting heavily.

Instead of slowing down, Rodney began to run even faster. "Catch me," he yelled, sticking his tongue out at his sister. He came to another corner, rounded it, and disappeared from her sight. She arrived at the corner only seconds after him, but when she got there her twin was gone.

Slowing down, Aimee continued to walk in the direction she had seen him go. "Rodney," she shouted, turning her head so she could be heard up and down the street, "this isn't funny." She scanned the area carefully, searching for some sign of him. Her face grew red and she yelled even louder, trying to sound as authoritative as their mother. Pausing beneath an old maple tree she repeated herself. "I said this isn't funny, Rodney. You come out of hiding this minute."

"If you say so," came Rodney's voice from overhead.

Aimee looked up in time to see her brother, who had been sitting on a thick branch of the tree, let go of his perch and descend upon her. He grabbed her around the waist as he dropped, using his momentum to drag her down onto the grass with him. Twisting so that he was on top, Rodney pinned his sister's hands behind her back.

"Stop it or I'll tell," she said, struggling to break free.

Rodney laughed. "How can you tell if I'm holding you captive?"

"You can't keep me here forever."

Rodney wrinkled his nose as he considered this. She was right. Eventually he would have to let her go, and then she would tell on him. He was in enough trouble at home already because of his last report card. His only hope was to make peace with her while he still had the chance. "All right," he said as he helped her to her feet. "I was just joking anyway."

Aimee straightened her clothes in as dignified a manner as possible and looked him in the eye. "I'm still telling."

"You're such a baby."

"I'm twelve years old, the same as you."

"But you're still a baby."

"Am not."

"Are too."

"Not."

"Too."

"Not."

Rodney thought things over. "If you're not such a baby, then prove it."

"How?"

Rodney looked up and down the street for an idea. His eyes finally rested on the Murillo house two doors down. "If you have enough guts to sneak with me into the Murillos' and steal an apple from the tree in their back yard, then I'll admit that you're not a baby. Otherwise, you might just as well go crying back to mommy and tell her that you need your diaper changed cuz you got pushed down."

"You know we're not supposed to do that," Aimee protested. "Mr. Murillo doesn't like anyone on his land. Billie Dale got grounded just last week because he was caught climbing that tree. I don't want to get grounded and I don't think you do either."

"Stop being such a baby. Billie got grounded because his parents told him not to climb the tree and he went and did it anyway. But we're not going to climb the tree. We're going to climb to the roof of the garage to get to the apples."

"It's still the same thing."

"No it isn't. Has anyone ever told us not to climb on the roof? No. Only the tree. So if we go on top of the roof to get the apples we're not doing anything that we've been told not to. Right?"

"Well, I guess not," Aimee admitted, "but I know that Mr. Murillo wouldn't like it, so we probably still shouldn't."

"You're just scared, baby. I'm going. Are you going with me, or are you gonna stay here and cry?"

"I guess so," Aimee said, against her better instincts. "But just remember that it was your idea and not mine."

"Great. Now follow me and keep quiet."

They walked quietly down the street, trying to look as innocent as possible. When they were sure that no one was around to see, they ran into the yard of the house next door to the Murillo's. They knew that they were in no danger of being caught there because the owner was out west on vacation, so they walked more confidently to the back of the house. Then, to Aimee's surprise, Rodney walked straight for what appeared to be a solid wooden fence covered with bushes. In reality, though, the bushes covered up a hole just big enough for the two twelve-year-olds to squeeze through. Climbing through the hole, they found themselves right in the middle of the Murillos' back yard.

"We'll have to be real quiet now, Aimee," said Rodney in a whisper.

"Okay," she answered. Her heart was pounding and she knew that she was too frightened to talk much anyway.

With Rodney in the lead, they made their way to the garage and then circled around it until they found a pile of old boxes that were stacked nearly as high as the garage itself. Rodney went first, climbing the boxes and swinging onto the roof so expertly that Aimee knew it wasn't his first time here. After watching what he did, she followed. Although she wasn't as graceful as her brother, she made it to the top without incident and soon they were both standing on the roof looking down on the Murillo back yard. Walking carefully to the other side of the garage, Rodney reached out and plucked two apples from a branch that stretched near the roof.

"Yummmmmmm," he said, taking a bite out of one and handing the other to his sister. "This is the best apple I've ever eaten."

Aimee took a bite out of hers and then crinkled her nose in disgust, spitting it back out in a big hurry. "Yuck. This apple is sour. You are only pretending to like it because you know we're not supposed to eat it. Just remember what happened to Adam and Eve when they ate their forbidden fruit."

Rodney looked away, pretending to ignore her, and then began to laugh. "Look over there, Aimee," he said, pointing toward the Murillo house. On the small roof over the back porch someone had left a Jack O'Lantern. The face had once been carved to make it look scary, but since Halloween was weeks ago and because it had been so warm the last couple of days, its face had collapsed inwards making it look silly.

"They must have forgotten all about it," Rodney suggested. "You're right about these apples being too gross to eat. Let's see if we can hit the pumpkin with them."

"I don't think that's a very good idea."

"I bet you're saying that because you know you're just a girl and your aim isn't as good as mine."

"You know I can throw every bit as good as you," Aimee told him. Rodney was always getting her to do things by saying he was better than her because he was a boy and she was a girl. It was really unfair of him and not even true, but he did it anyway.

Against her better judgment, Aimee succumbed to Rodney's taunting and gripped the apple in her right hand. Pulling her arm back, she took aim at the target and released the apple. She had judged the distance right, but the angle was a little off and the apple sailed just to the left of the pumpkin, thudded against the side of the porch and dropped to the ground.

"I knew you couldn't hit it," Rodney said, laughing.

"Let's see you do any better," challenged Aimee. Her voice was thick with anger.

Rodney pushed her gently aside and then stretched to loosen up his arm. "Now watch how a real pro does it."

He drew back his arm, took careful aim, and snapped it forward throwing the fruit as hard as he could. The apple flew so fast that there was no arc whatsoever. It traveled in a straight line and hit the pumpkin exactly where the nose had been carved. Because the pumpkin had been rotting in the sun for a month, the apple plowed through it like water. Still traveling briskly, the apple then smashed into a stained glass window that was behind the pumpkin. There was a loud crash, and thousands of tiny shards of colored glass flew in every direction. Aimee let out a little scream and Rodney's face turned white.

"Run!" Rodney yelled, and they both jumped down from the garage as fast as they could. Behind them they heard a door open and saw Mrs. Murillo coming out to see what had happened.

CHAPTER TWO
Contact

"Hurry," Rodney told his sister. "In here." He scrambled through the hole in the fence as quickly as he could, and Aimee followed. Once on the other side the twins rested, pressing as close to the fence as possible.

Rodney was all out of breath from the mad dash to safety. "Do you think she saw us?"

"I doubt it," Aimee answered. "We got out of there pretty fast. Better stay here a few more minutes to make sure it's safe, though."

As they waited, a sudden thought hit Rodney. "You're not going to tell on me, are you?"

Aimee considered the question carefully before answering. "I don't know, Rodney. I don't want you to get in trouble, and I know you didn't do it on purpose, but it was still a very bad thing that you did. That window looked like it cost a lot of money, and it won't be fair if Mr. Murillo has to pay for it himself. I don't know what to do."

Rodney didn't like that answer. To show his displeasure, he placed his sister in a headlock and rubbed the top of her head briskly with his knuckles.

"Cut that out, it hurts," she protested, trying all the while to wiggle free of her brother's grasp.

"It'll hurt a lot more if you tell on me," Rodney said as Aimee finally broke free. "Remember that."

They fell into silence, each thinking their own thoughts, and sat there for fifteen or twenty minutes or more. Carefully poking his head over the fence, Rodney scanned the area. "I think it's safe," he said. "Let's go home."

They got up and made their way back to their own street as casually as possible. By the time they reached their house they found that it was already time to eat, so they went right upstairs to clean up for dinner.

"What are you going to do?" Rodney whispered as he soaped his hands up.

"I don't know," Aimee answered just as quietly as she rinsed her own hands off.

Rinsing the soap from his hands, Rodney shut the water off. "Don't forget," he said as he reached for a towel. "You were there too."

"And don't you forget," Aimee responded, this time a little too loudly, "you were the one who broke the window, not me."

"What are you two whispering about?" their mother asked as they came out of the washroom.

"Nothing," the twins chorused, each giving the other a suspicious look.

"Then hurry up and get seated. Your father's carving the turkey he baked right now, and he wants us to eat together as a family. You know how much he loves Thanksgiving."

Saying no more about the incident or anything else, the twins moved into the dining room and took their places at the table. As their parents brought the food in from the kitchen, Rodney continued to watch Aimee with a worried eye, but not a word was spoken. Finally, everything was on the table and they were ready to begin. Rodney started to grab for the stuffing but was stopped by his father.

"Patience, boy. There'll be plenty of time to eat in a moment, but don't you think we should first thank Our Father in Heaven for blessing us with all this wonderful food?"

"Yes, sir," Rodney muttered under his breath as he pulled his hand away from the stuffing bowl.

"Good," their father said, turning to face his daughter. "Would you like to do us the honor of saying grace this afternoon, Aimee?"

Aimee was shocked and a little bit surprised. Father always said grace for the family on special occasions himself. Ordinarily she would have felt proud to be given the honor, but instead she was feeling guilty. While they were preparing to eat this wonderful dinner, the Murillos were probably still picking up pieces of broken glass. She didn't want to tell on Rodney, but she knew that she couldn't lie or keep things hidden from God. Her parents were waiting for her, so, like it or not, she had to begin. Bowing her head, she held her hands in front of her and clasped her fingers together.

"Dear Lord," she said, "I'd like to thank You for all the really good food on the table and ask You to make sure that we get to keep on eating like this. And please bless all of us here and forgive us for our sins and help us to not sin any more so that we're able to become better people more worthy of Your love. And especially forgive Rodney for … OUCH!"

Aimee jumped up from the table and rubbed her shin where Rodney had kicked her, and just as quickly their father was up on his feet as well. He grabbed Rodney firmly by the arm and pulled the boy out of his seat. "Go ahead, Aimee. Forgive Rodney for what?"

Aimee was in tears knowing that Rodney would be punished if she told what had happened, but she was too frightened not to tell the truth. "I was going to ask God to forgive Rodney for throwing an apple through the Murillo porch window, but…"

"That's all I need to know. Sit down now and eat your dinner. And as for you," Father yelled as he turned to face Rodney, "you can forget all about the turkey and the stuffing and especially that banana cream pie that you're always pestering me to make. There will be no dinner for you. I'm disappointed, young man. Very disappointed. If you won't let Aimee ask God to forgive you, then maybe you need to do it yourself. I want you to march straight upstairs to your room so you can be alone with Him for a few hours. That means no television, no radio and no computer. I want you to spend your time thinking about what you did wrong and how you could have acted to avoid this whole situation. And later we'll go over to the Murillos' house so you can apologize to them and make arrangements to pay them back. Do you understand?"

Rodney muttered something, but his voice was so quiet that no one could hear him.

"I said do you understand?"

"I said yes," Rodney snapped back.

Father pointed toward the staircase. "Now go."

Rodney walked slowly over to the stairs and even slower up them. His head was hung between his shoulders and he was all stooped over. He had begun to cry a little, but he didn't know if he was crying because he had done something wrong or because he had gotten caught. When he got to the top of the stairs he scurried into his bedroom and threw himself onto the bed. He had tried to fight the tears before when he was still where his family could see him, but now that he was alone he didn't care. He let them flow freely.

He lay there for such a long time that his pillowcase became soaked with the salty tears. He was hungry and his stomach was growling, but he was determined not to go downstairs and beg forgiveness. He tried to forget about the food, but it wasn't easy. He had been looking forward to Thanksgiving dinner and the banana cream pie for weeks, and now he wasn't going to get any. It was his favorite kind and they usually had it only twice a year, at Thanksgiving and at Christmas. He didn't know if he could wait another month before getting a slice.

Finally, he realized that the only way to forget about his stomach was to do something. Since he wasn't able to use the computer, he decided to do a little drawing by hand and pulled out his art supplies. He started to draw a unicorn, but all of his books on horse anatomy were downstairs. He didn't want to chance meeting his father again, so he crumpled up that piece of paper and started work on another.

Rodney made several other attempts, but he wasn't happy with anything he had drawn, and soon his trash can was full of ripped up and crinkled papers. He was about to give up and go back to his bed to sulk some more when his eyes made contact with the drawing he had made earlier, before Aimee came and talked him into going out to play. Picking it up, he looked it over carefully. He liked it. It was one of the best that he had ever done, but something seemed to be missing. After a couple of minutes of close study he realized what. Normally when he drew landscapes that was all he drew, but this picture cried out for more. It needed a person.

Rodney decided to put this person in the foreground of the drawing, in front of the hills so he didn't block the stream or the village that it eventually flowed near. He intention was that this person would be a happy farmer, but when he put his pencil to the paper it seemed to take on a life of its own. His pencil danced across the page and he drew without thinking, letting his instincts guide him.

When he was finished it was not a happy farmer but a somber, important-looking man that was standing on the page before him. Rodney colored the man in and then held the drawing up to inspect it. Tall and lean, the man looked back at Rodney with dark, intelligent eyes and a very serious expression on his face. The boy smiled as he studied the paper. This drawing felt more right than any he had ever created before.

Finished, he placed the drawing to the side so he could move on with something else. Before he could decide what that something else might be, he was distracted by a deep voice calling his name.

"Rodney, we need your help," the voice said in a low, desperate tone.

The young boy looked around the room. The TV and computer were both still shut off. He couldn't see anyone. This made him nervous, and he tried to calm down by telling himself that it was only the wind or his imagination. Before he could fully convince himself of this he heard the voice repeat its plea for help. Rodney began to get scared. He scanned the room more frantically, but look as hard as he might he still couldn't see anything.

"I'm down here, Rodney," the voice told him. "In your picture."

Still frightened, Rodney looked down at the piece of paper he had set aside only moments ago. He squinted to inspect the drawing he had so recently completed. What he saw surprised him and he almost let out a scream. The man that he had drawn was still there, just like Rodney had made him, except now he was moving around like a cartoon. As if that wasn't shocking enough, the man went one step further. He talked.

"Don't be frightened," the man told him. "I'm not here to harm you, just to beseech your succor. Please listen carefully. Although your drawing has allowed me to broach the distance between our two worlds, it is difficult for me to maintain contact and I can't do it for very long."

"Who are you?" stuttered Rodney. He had meant to sound brave and sure of himself, but the quivering in his voice revealed his fear.

"I am Yenspetsnicksnack from the Land of Daak, Rodney. Your land."

"What do you mean?"

The cartoon man froze for a moment before responding. "I know that this may be difficult for you to understand right now, Rodney, but Daak exists because of you and your art, and its people are in serious jeopardy. You see, Haeron, the evil sorceress, has established her dominion in our glorious realm. She is pernicious, Rodney, and has begun a reign of unparalleled terror that threatens us all with perpetual slavery and ruination. Already three-fourths of the land has fallen, and it is only a matter of time before she will defeat us all."

"Can't you do anything to stop her?" Rodney asked, though to be honest he wasn't all that sure he understood everything Yenspetsnicksnack had told him. Some of the words the man had used were too big for Rodney.

"Alone, no, dear Rodney. Her power is too strong. There is only one person who can extricate us, only one person who can relieve us from this miserable existence. He who owns the land. He who controls our destiny. He who lives so that, through him, we all may live. That person is you, Rodney. We must have your help if our world is to be delivered."

"I don't understand anything you're saying," Rodney interrupted. "Why do you talk so funny?"

"Ah, please allow me to apologize. I am the mayor of Foran Village here in Daak, and in my political undertakings I am used to using big words and complex phrases designed to confuse others and make them think that I'm smarter than I really am. As a politician it is expected of me.

"What I am trying to say is that there is an evil sorceress who is taking over our land, and without your help we will all be her slaves forever. You are the only one who can help us because Daak is your own private world created through your art. Don't feel badly if you can't understand everything that I am telling you because I don't really understand it all myself. But I do know this: we won't be able to survive without you. Won't you help us, please?"

By this time Rodney's fear was becoming fascination. He thought about his options for a little while, weighing the punishment he might receive from his father if caught with the thrill of going to a magical world. It didn't take him too long to make a decision and his heart was racing with excitement as he answered. "Of course I'll help. What do I have to do?"

"Absolutely nothing. I'll do all the work," answered the cartoon man. "Now just reach out your hand and close your eyes and the spell which allowed me to contact you will also permit you to enter our world."

Rodney did what he was told. With his eyes closed he was unable to see the blinding rainbow of light that flooded into the room from the drawing. He was unable to see first a finger and then a whole hand reach out from the drawing and take hold of his own in a magical embrace. He was unable to see the mystical aura that slowly grew all about him, enveloping his body. And most of all, he was unable to see when Aimee entered the room carrying a tray full of food.

"Rodney, Mom said that I should bring some dinner up to you and..." she began, but her words were cut off as she pushed the door open and saw what was happening. Dropping the tray to the floor with a crash, she screamed and shielded her eyes with her hands to protect them from the intense light. Carefully reopening her eyes, she squinted through two spread fingers. Her brother was being slowly pulled into a weird hole on his drawing table! Without a thought for her own personal safety, she lunged forward and grabbed a hold of his arm. She tugged, but whatever had a hold of Rodney was tugging harder. The force on the other end was too powerful. She latched her other hand on the bookcase hoping to gain some leverage, but that didn't do any good. The bookcase came crashing down around them scattering books in every direction. They were still being pulled in.

Hearing the noise, their mother called up the stairs demanding to know what was going on.

There was no one left in the room to answer her.

CHAPTER THREE
Foran Village

Rodney opened his eyes. The man he had created was holding his hand, but he was no longer just a drawing. He was now made of flesh and blood, as real as Rodney himself. The ground, the sky, everything was as real as any the boy had ever seen. There was nothing to hint at the fact that, mere moments ago, this had all been a drawing. Rodney had a million questions to ask, but before he could get any of them out, Aimee started crying.

That startled Rodney and surprised Yenspetsnicksnack for neither, up until that point, had noticed that Aimee was with them. And because she had come into the room at the last moment she had no idea what was going on. She was completely lost.

Rodney introduced Yenspetsnicksnack to his sister, who did his best to calm her down before explaining to her what had happened. Within minutes she knew as much about the situation as her brother, which is to say not very much at all.

When he was done telling Aimee what he had already conveyed to Rodney, Yenspetsnicksnack suggested that they head toward his house. He pointed the way, but only managed a couple of steps before his legs began to shake and his face twisted in pain. With a great deal of effort, he lowered himself to the ground.

"What's wrong?" both children asked as they knelt by his side.

Yenspetsnicksnack clutched his midsection and gritted his teeth. "I purchased the spell to transport you here from a magician who lived in another part of Daak," he explained through deep breaths. "He told me that there might be a painful side effect to the spell, and I guess this is it. It's only supposed to be temporary, though, and I should be all right in a few minutes. I just need to rest a bit."

"Why didn't the magician bring us here himself?" Rodney wanted to know.

Yens hesitated a second as if he didn't know the answer. "Because," he finally answered, struggling to get the words out through the pain, "he could not. The evil sorceress is very powerful, you see, and soon after she established her dominion she rounded up all the wizards and witches and other magic users in the Land of Daak and made slaves out of them. The ones that resisted slavery were all put to death, their heads shrunken and hung throughout her castle as decorations. I was fortunate enough to buy this spell before the magician who sold it to me was captured and killed."

"Yenspiet…" began Rodney, but he stopped abruptly as he was having difficulty pronouncing the name. "Yinspets…" he started again, pausing as he realized he was having the same trouble. Giving up, he said, "Do you mind if I just call you 'Yens'? I can't seem to say your full name right."

"Not at all, good sir," came the reply. "Not at all. For the pleasure of your august company and the companionship of your beautiful sister I would brave the most trying of difficulties and allow myself to be degraded in any way you please."

From the uncomprehending look on Rodney's face, Yenspetsnicksnack realized that he was talking over the young boy's head again and reworded his speech. "Of course you may call me Yens, but remember that I am granting you a concession by allowing this. My mother would turn over in her grave if she knew I was allowing my given name of Yenspetsnicksnack to be shortened from its glorious length, but seeing as this is your world and I am your faithful servant, how can I refuse?"

"Then Yens it is," Rodney said. Then, turning to his sister, he added, "I guess it looks like were really going to have that adventure that I talked about this morning. Let's go see the Sorceress."

"Not so fast," Yens warned. "First we must be sure to map out our journey carefully and prepare our packs to ensure that we have suitable clothing and enough food to last us until we reach our destination. We'll need weapons to defend ourselves, and we must be skilled with the weapons we choose. It will be a week or more before we're ready to begin."

Aimee didn't like the idea of spending any more time in Daak than she had to, and the thought of it being a week before they could even begin their quest did not please her at all. Rodney may have agreed to come to this world, but she certainly didn't, and she wanted to get home as quickly as she could. And she was not afraid to say so.

"Why do we have to do all that? In *The Wizard of Oz* Dorothy just grabbed her basket and headed down the Yellow Brick Road. She didn't spend days in Munchkinland getting ready for her journey and she still managed to defeat the wicked witch and save the Emerald City. Why can't we do the same, march right up to the sorceress and challenge her. In school Mrs. Herr says that good is stronger than evil…"

"It said that on *Star Trek* too," Rodney interrupted, trying to be helpful. Aimee shot her brother a dirty look and continued.

"Since good is stronger than evil, and since we are the good guys and the sorceress is the evil one, why can't we do what Dorothy did and just go save Daak?"

"I know not this Dorothy that you speak of," Yens said, measuring his words carefully, "but I do know Haeron. Were we to do as you suggest, her armies would cut us to pieces before we came within twenty miles of her fortress, good intentions or no. Or worse yet, they might let us live only to enslave us. And if we do not turn out to be useful slaves she will slowly and painfully chop off pieces from our bodies and make us watch as she feeds them to her pets – horrific monsters like dragons and griffins.

"Goodness alone will not guarantee our protection, dear Aimee. Consider your own not too distant past and an evil man named Adolph Hitler. True, the forces of good eventually stopped him, but not before he killed countless innocents. No, if we are to be successful in this mission we will require careful planning. And assistance. Remember when I stated that the dark sorceress had killed or enslaved all the magic wielders on Daak? Well, I've been informed by a spy within Haeron's fortress that one magician has eluded her grasp. His name is Archimagus and he is perhaps the most powerful magician in this entire world. We will need his help to defeat the sorceress, but we have to find him before we can ask him to assist us. He has gone into hiding and no one has heard from him in years. We will have to locate him before we can do anything else."

Yens stretched his arms above his head. "But enough about this for now. Surely you are both tired and hungry, I know I am. Let us return to Foran Village for food and rest and we will discuss the situation in more detail when our needs have been attended to." Yens carefully pulled himself back to his feet. Stretching again, he smiled to let the children know that the pain was gone and then motioned toward the village in the distance.

* * *

Entering Foran Village was like stepping more than a century into the past. The buildings were simple structures made of wood or stone. Very few of them looked big enough to have more than three rooms, and not a single one had a second story. Only a couple of the houses had ever been painted, and on those the paint was old and chipping. With the exception of the main street, which was lined with stone, all the roads were dirt. Here and there a board was set on the ground to allow people to walk over particularly muddy areas, but there was no sidewalk to speak of. The village looked like an odd mixture of styles, from medieval Europe to the old American west.

The people were just as dirty and as strange as their village, and as the twins walked through the town it became obvious to them that they were being avoided. No one talked to them. No one made eye contact with them. Most of the natives, in fact, seemed to purposely cross to the other side of the street or duck into nearby doorways as the group approached. Rodney and Aimee also noticed that no one in Foran Village smiled, not even the children. They all looked sad. Even their clothing looked sad. Everyone moved slowly and wore shaggy garments of black or gray. There wasn't a happy color or face to be seen anywhere in town streets.

As Yens led them around a corner, they approached what could only be described as a playground. Even though there were no swings, slides or basketball hoops to mark it as such, several children clustered within it and tossed a ball around. Here was the only place that they saw people having fun, but that didn't last for long. A young boy about the same age as the twins reached for the ball as it was thrown to him but missed. It bounced off his fingertips and landed directly at Aimee's feet. The boy scurried after it and started to smile when he saw Aimee, but then he stopped suddenly in his tracks. His smile quickly changed to a look of terror and he bolted in the opposite direction, rounding a corner and disappearing from sight. All the children that were at the playground scattered, in fact, fleeing in every direction. Within seconds the entire street was deserted. Shrugging her shoulders, Aimee scooped up the ball, looked at it briefly, and stuffed it into her pocket.

"Why is everyone avoiding us?" she wanted to know. "Don't they know that we're here to help them?"

"You must understand what life is like for them here on Daak, my dear," Yens responded, his answer sounding to Aimee like it had been rehearsed. "Ever since Haeron took over it has been a struggle for them to survive. Even though Foran is one of the few places still free of her direct influence, her grasp can be felt. Many of our people have relatives in other villages that have already been captured, and even those who don't know that it's just a matter of time before her armies try to take this town. Her spies have probably already established themselves here, and no one knows who can be trusted and who can't. Being strangers, the people are naturally afraid of you because they don't know who you are. They fear that you might be her servants."

Rodney thought about this. "Couldn't you tell them who we are? After all, you are their mayor. Won't they believe you if you tell them that we're friendly and here to help?"

"Perhaps," Yens agreed, nodding his head. "But if I tell my people who you really are, any spies that that sorceress has here would also know. And if Haeron knew who you really were she would have her assassins dispatched immediately to kill you both.

Aimee and Rodney shuddered at that thought.

Yens continued. "Our best bet is secrecy. No one should know anything about what we are trying to do and no one should know who the two of you are. I don't want either one of you to talk to anyone without getting my permission first, and if someone tries to get information out of you tell him nothing. The fewer who know anything about us, the better off we are."

They turned another corner and Yens pointed to a building looming directly in front of them. "Welcome to Yenspetsnicksnack Manor," he said with more than a hint of pride. "A humble little home, but it's all mine."

Humble was not a word that either of the twins would have used to describe the building. In contrast to all the other homes in the village, in contrast to all the homes in the town where Aimee and Rodney lived, in fact, this one was luxurious. It towered above every other building in the village and took up about five acres of land. Where most of the other residences were in various states of disrepair, this one was in immaculate condition. Every window was made of hand-painted stained glass, and the doors were all decorated with ornate brass fixtures. The land behind the house stretched so far that the children couldn't see where it ended.

"It's lovely," Aimee said as they approached the main entrance. "But so big. Do you live here all by yourself?"

Yens smiled. "Yes. I have several servants, but I am the sole master of the house."

As the trio got closer, the two front doors to the mansion opened, each held by a well-dressed manservant. Like the people of the village, the doormen spoke not a word and refused to look at the children as they passed. Instead they stared directly at the ground until Yens and the twins walked past them, at which time they silently and simultaneously closed the doors. In the foyer, a third servant made his presence known. This one, a funny little man who seemed very strange and nervous, did speak.

Running up to them, he bowed before Yenspetsnicksnack. "What is your pleasure, sir?"

Yens made a motion with his hands and the little man stood straight. "We have guests, Ho-Don," Yens then said with authority as he indicated Aimee and Rodney. "See to it that their rooms are prepared for them."

With a nod the little man scurried off to carry out his orders. When he was gone, Yens looked at the twins. "Are you hungry?"

Aimee had eaten well at the Thanksgiving dinner prior to being transported unexpectedly to Daak, but Rodney hadn't had a bite since breakfast and was starving. He let Yens know that without hesitation.

Ho-Don came running back into the Foyer. "The rooms are being prepared, master," he said as he bowed.

"Excellent. My young guests are hungry. See to their needs and then put them to bed." Turning to face the twins, he continued. "Ho-Don will show you to your rooms and fix you whatever you desire. Stay with him and do what he says. After you eat I suggest you go right to sleep. We begin our preparations tomorrow, and you are going to need your rest. For safety's sake you will speak to no one but Ho-Don and myself. Now if you will excuse me, I have to attend to some mayoral business. I will see you first thing in the morning."

Ho-Don bowed to the children, but his eyes followed Yens as he disappeared into the depths of the house. "This way, please, young master and mistress," he said as soon as Yens was out of sight. Following the little man's lead, the twins climbed the set of stairs opposite them and then walked down a long hallway lined with elegant and colorful paintings. Aimee wanted to look at each picture, but Ho-Don quickly led the children into a large bedroom that was beautifully decorated and at least twice as large as either of their rooms back home. Rodney ran straight to the bed and jumped on it while Aimee stood and gaped at the splendor of everything in the room, from the curtains to the bed sheets.

As she was looking about, the little man opened a door that was next to a very ornate, deep cherry dresser. Inside, Aimee could see another room exactly like the one they were in. One for her and one for her brother.

"Now what can I do to ease your hunger?" Ho-Don asked.

"Nothing for me, thank you," Aimee said as politely as possible. A shock of blonde hair fell across her eyes and she reached up to brush it back with her hand.

"And you, young master?"

Rodney stopped jumping on the bed and thought the matter over. "I can have anything I want?"

"Anything."

A mischievous grin formed on the boy's face and he smacked his lips. "In that case I think I'll have a bowl of chocolate pudding, a plate of peanut butter cookies and a bag of potato chips. And for dessert I'd like a hot fudge sundae."

To the surprise of both twins, Ho-Don turned without question and left to fill Rodney's order. When he was gone, Aimee turned and pointed a finger at her brother. "Mom and Dad would never let you eat all that junk at once, especially in place of dinner."

Rodney leaned back on the bed and tucked a pillow under his head. "Mom and Dad aren't here."

CHAPTER FOUR
Preparations

As Aimee looked on in disbelief, her brother finished his hot fudge sundae and ordered a second. He ate four large bowls of ice cream, in fact, before he was finished. And after licking the fourth bowl clean he complained of a bellyache.

"Serves you right," Aimee said as she took a tissue and wiped away some ice cream that had missed his mouth and was beginning to dry on his chin.

Ho-Don bowed low to the two of them. "If you will be requiring nothing else, I will take my leave." Then, without waiting for an answer, he spun around on his heels and walked into the hallway.

The door shut behind Ho-Don with a click, which was followed almost immediately by a second click. Curious, Aimee crossed the room and tried the handle. "We're locked in."

The door in the other bedroom was locked as well, which made Aimee nervous, but Rodney took it in stride. Pushing the thick cream curtains aside, the twins opened a bedroom window. It over-looked a lush garden filled with all kinds of wonderful flowers that could be seen clearly in the glow of Daak's twin moons. Ignoring the garden and the lovely countryside beyond, the twins looked straight down. "Too far to jump," Rodney said, and Aimee nodded her head in agreement.

Frustrated, Aimee put her elbows on the windowsill and looked up at the sky. The two moons caught her attention, and she pointed them out to Rodney. He slid next to her and they silently gazed at the heavens together.

"I don't get it," Aimee said after a while, breaking the silence of the moment. "If we're here to help why are we being treated like prisoners?"

Rodney shrugged his shoulders but didn't say a word. He was still distracted by the stars. One of them began to move. It shot across the sky and then burned itself out near the horizon. "Shooting star," he said. "Make a wish."

"I wish we were home."

Another light moved across the sky and then faded away. "Didn't work, we're still here," Rodney said. "It's kind of dumb to wish on them anyway. Dad says they're not really stars falling, just space rocks burning up from friction when they hit the atmosphere."

He pushed himself away from the window and looked toward the doorway leading into the other bedroom. "Maybe we should go to bed like we were told and get some sleep. Yens said that tomorrow is going to be a long day so we'll probably need it. I'm sure he'll explain everything in the morning."

Rodney stood up and went straight into the other room, blowing out the candles that served as light but leaving the door between the rooms open. Within minutes he was asleep and Aimee could hear him snoring.

* * *

Morning came.

Aimee shifted, her eyelids vibrating rapidly to indicate that she was dreaming. In her dream she saw the boy from the playground. His ball rolled to a stop at her feet and he bent down to get it. He looked up and their eyes met. A warm glow came over her and she smiled. He was smiling too. He reached his hand out and she extended hers. Before their hands made contact, however, a man materialized between them and the smile melted away from the boy's face. He screamed. He was still screaming in her mind when she felt herself being pulled from the dream.

She opened her eyes, blinking to adjust to the light. At first she was confused, disoriented. Already the events of the dream were fading from her mind, but the emotional effect remained. She still felt the boy's anxiety.

Ignoring everything else, she stared blankly ahead trying to reconstruct the details of her dream. Just as she was piecing elements together, a pair of hands grabbed her by the shoulders and shook her. Aimee's attention focused on Rodney, the shaker, and the dream was lost.

"Snap out of it," he yelled. "We've got to get out of here fast."

"Why? What's wrong?"

"Can't you smell that?"

Aimee sniffed deeply. "Bacon and eggs?"

"Yep," Rodney agreed, nodding his head excitedly. "Scrambled and boiled eggs. And bacon and pancakes and sausage and hash browns and French toast. It smells like the best breakfast ever made. We gotta get out of here and find it."

Aimee stretched, yawning. As she did her best to straighten out the wrinkles caused by sleeping in her clothes, Rodney ran to the door and tried to turn the knob. "It's still locked," he whined. "And I'm starved."

"How can you be starved? You ate enough junk food last night for six people. You shouldn't be hungry again for at least a week."

Rodney tried to think of a smart reply to his sister's comment. When he couldn't, he decided on the next best action. He stuck out his tongue.

"It doesn't matter anyway," Aimee added. "Hungry or not, we're not going anywhere until someone lets us out."

As if on cue, the door to the room swung wide open. "The master would like me to inform you that breakfast is just about ready," Ho-Don told them. "If you will follow me I will show you where you can wash up."

Rodney licked his lips and thought about the food. "We don't need to wash up," he said. Before he could get any more out he was interrupted by Aimee's hand slapping the back of his head. "But of course we will," he added, glaring at his twin.

Once clean, they were led into a dining room so large it belonged in a palace. The table was loaded and Aimee was surprised to note that Rodney had guessed exactly which foods would be served. There was a large platter of scrambled eggs, still steaming hot, placed right next to equally large platters of sausage and bacon. The pancakes and French toast were stacked twelve inches deep and a big dish of hash brown potatoes sat between them. Next to each plate, a small cup held a hard boiled egg and there were condiments of every kind scattered across the table; several different flavors of syrup, jams and jellies, butter and margarine, almost any kind of topping you could think of. There were also several pitchers on the table, each containing milk or a different kind of juice. In short, there was enough food to feed a small nation, but there were only settings for three.

Yenspetsnicksnack came running into the dining hall and slid right into his seat. He motioned for the children to sit down as well.

Aimee sat politely, waiting for Yens to say grace. Instead, he just started shoveling food onto his plate and soon Rodney was doing the same. Within seconds their plates were each heaped full of food, eggs spilling over into potatoes, potatoes covering pancakes and meat. "I hope you like everything," Yens said after swallowing a mouthful of eggs/potatoes/sausage."

Rodney was busy pouring thick strawberry syrup over everything on his plate. "I'm sure I will," he finally answered. Setting the syrup down, he pulled a forkful of food that was now no more than an unrecognizable mush from his plate. "Our Uncle Ron says that if food is free, it's gotta be good." Pushing the fork into his mouth, Rodney chewed on the mixture and smiled.

Meanwhile, having decided that grace was not going to be said, Aimee placed a modest portion of eggs, one piece of French toast and two links of sausage on her plate. Before talking a bite, she looked over to Yens. "Why did you lock us in our rooms last night?"

Yens held up one finger. His mouth was full of food and he wanted to swallow before speaking. "I did it to protect you," he finally said, after chewing for nearly a minute. As if that were explanation enough, he turned back to his plate and shoved another forkful of food into his mouth.

"Protect us? By treating us like prisoners?"

Again she had to wait for Yens to finish his food before he was ready to speak. "You're hardly prisoners, my dear, but you can't be allowed to run around unsupervised either, especially during a period of Heavenfall. I've done my best to keep your presence a secret, but we must remain careful. If the evil sorceress even suspects your existence on this world she will stop at nothing to capture or kill you. Until you have a better understanding of the situation I must insist on keeping constant track of your whereabouts. Believe me, I only have your best interests in mind."

"And what if some emergency were to come up like a fire? Suppose our lived depended on us getting out of the rooms as quickly as possible? We couldn't do that if we were locked in."

"I hadn't thought of that," Yens admitted, "but I'm afraid the greater danger still lies outside the rooms. I'll tell you what. Ho-Don's room is directly across the hall from your own. I'll have a bell installed. Ring it, and Ho-Don will be there to let you out within moments. All right?"

Aimee nodded her head but she still wasn't satisfied. Yens had said nothing to make her feel less like a prisoner. She picked quietly at her food for the rest of the meal as Rodney and Yens stuffed themselves like pigs.

* * *

As soon as breakfast was over, Ho-Don went to work cleaning the table, which was remarkably easy to do because, between Yens and Rodney, nearly every scrap of food had been eaten.

Yens, meanwhile, led the twins into his private study. Bookcases with shelves filled to capacity lined every wall in the large room. An oversized desk sprawled comfortably along the back wall and four tables clustered before it like saplings in the shade of a giant oak.

Yens sat the children down at one of these desks and pulled a very large book from one of the shelves. Opening it to a pre-marked page, he said, "This is an atlas of the known territories on the land of Daak. I want you to familiarize yourselves with the charts that I've noted. I've mapped out our intended route to Frieer."

"Frieer?" questioned Aimee.

"The frozen land to the north, rumored home of the Hidden People. They can be powerful allies if we are able to locate them, and it's likely that they are giving refuge to Archimagus. Look this over and feel free to examine any other book in here. Much of our journey there will be through wild and mainly unexplored lands and it will be very dangerous. The more we know the safer we'll be. Once you've finished with these I have several other volumes on the history and culture of Frieer, as well as those of other peoples we are likely to encounter along the way."

Aimee studied the books excitedly. Rodney glanced at them with reluctance. As they looked the maps over, Yens placed the other books on the table and then excused himself, claiming to have other business to attend to.

As soon as Yens had departed, Rodney got up and started pacing around the room. "This is boring. It's too much like school and I hate it."

"You better learn to like it fast, Rodney," Aimee replied, trying to sound grown up. "Knowing what's in these books may save our lives."

Ignoring her, he tried the door. Neither of the children was surprised that the handle was locked. While Aimee read, Rodney curled up in a chair and slept until it was time for lunch.

After lunch the children were led back into the study where Rodney paced for an hour or so as Aimee read. Then, while looking at the titles out of boredom, he noticed one called *Fighting Styles of the Truculans.*

The Truculans, he learned, were a warrior people who once lived somewhere to the south of Foran. Fierce and relentless, they had a highly developed sense of honor and justice and were feared and respected by everyone that ever encountered them. They ruled from their capital city, Sedes, and for more than a thousand years kept the peace and acted as the voice of reason on Daak. They were masters of every known weapon and would probably still be ruling Daak if Haeron hadn't invented the Volcanic Blast, a magical spell so powerful that it completely destroyed Sedes and everyone in it. In a matter of hours the reign of the Truculans came to an end and the evil tyranny of Haeron had begun. The hidden people of Frieer were rumored to be the descendants of those few Truculans who were fortunate enough to be away from Sedes when the blast hit. It is said that they will someday return and, with the help of their greatest king, reestablish Truculan rule over Daak.

Rodney read *Fighting Styles of the Truculans* with an intensity that Aimee had never before seen in her brother. When it was time to go to bed that night he took the book with him and stayed up until he had finished it. When the lights were finally out he fell right asleep, his snores echoing between the rooms and filling Aimee's wide-awake ears.

* * *

The next day was more to Rodney's liking, and Aimee enjoyed herself as well. There were no motor cars anywhere on Daak. With the exception of walking, horseback riding was the only practical method of traveling from one place to another.

Besides being dangerous, the journey to Frieer was going to be long. Walking would take months while riding would cut the trip to a matter of days. Because of this, the children were led by Ho-Don to the stable where they were each allowed to pick out one horse that would be theirs. Rodney chose a streamlined Arabian stallion with deep chestnut coloring while Aimee took a beautiful light tan Palomino with spotted markings.

The rest of the day was spent learning how to ride, or equestrian training as Yens called it. The twins were so interested that they continued straight on through lunch and had to be coerced into eating dinner. They both rushed though the meal in order to get back to their horses as quickly as possible and continued riding until dark.

"I think I'll name my horse Credalis," Rodney told his sister later that night. "It's a Truculan word meaning 'trusted friend'. How about you?"

"I don't know. I was thinking of calling him Ed, but next to Credalis Ed sounds so boring."

"Why Ed?"

Aimee shrugged her shoulders. "Because he kind of looks like Mr. Ed from TV I guess."

They stayed up for an hour trying to think of a better name, but after a long list of possibilities had been considered and rejected, Aimee decided to stay with Ed. That matter settled, they turned off the lights. Again, Rodney was asleep and snoring within minutes, but this time Aimee didn't hear it. She had fallen asleep first.

* * *

They both woke up extra early the following morning. Yens had kept his promise and had the bell installed, so the children had only to ring it in order to be released. Ho-Don came at once, bringing them fresh clothing, and once they were dressed they ran straight for the stable. Ed and Credalis were as glad to see their new masters as the twins were to see them, and they rode for an hour before being called for breakfast.

After eating they ran back to their horses where they rode until Ho-Don fetched them. Bringing them back into the house he led them through a hallway that they had never been down before. Stopping before an unmarked door he opened it but did not follow them in.

Inside was a large room with every kind of weapon imaginable covering the walls. Every kind, that is, except for firearms. Gunpowder had never been invented on Daak and, as a result, there were no guns on the entire world. Still, the people of Daak like those of earth had managed to create hundreds of other tools designed for the sole purpose of killing.

The floor of the room, unlike the walls, was completely barren and made of a soft, spongy material. Yens stood waiting in the middle of the room, a sword in his hand. "Welcome to phase two of your training," he said, lifting the sword in what seemed to be some form of military salute.

Then, without warning, he pointed the sword at Rodney and lunged, forcing its point squarely into the young boy's chest.

CHAPTER FIVE
Airia's Tale

Aimee screamed.

Rodney gasped and clutched his chest.

There was no blood.

Yens pulled the sword back and let it dangle at his side. He looked Rodney straight in the eye. "You're dead."

Rodney's heart was pumping furiously as he probed his chest with his fingers. "I don't feel dead."

Yens lifted the murder weapon and held it in front of the young boy. "This is a trick sword," He said as he pushed the point with the palm of his hand. The blade collapsed upon itself. "Had it been real it would have gone straight through your heart. You would be dead."

Aimee and Rodney both looked at the man, not knowing what to say. After a pause to let his lesson sink in, he continued in a loud and angry voice. "I told you that danger exists everywhere. You should constantly be prepared for it. You could have ducked out of the way when I lunged at you, but you didn't. You just stood there like a fool and let yourself get killed."

Yens reached out to place his arm around Rodney and continued in a more gentle tone. "I know I frightened you and I'm sorry, but it was the best way to get my point across." He poked Rodney with the tip of the trick sword. "No pun intended. Look, it comes down to this: You'll be of no use to me if you're dead. And you will certainly be of no use to yourself. What I want to work on today is self-defense. Here, now you take this sword and come at me the same way I came at you."

Rodney did as he was told and lunged the trick sword at Yens' chest. Instead of letting it hit him, though, Yens managed to step aside. Then, with Rodney's arm still extended, he chopped at the boy's wrist, forcing him to drop the sword.

"See how easy that was? That's what you should have done to me."

* * *

The rest of the day was spent with Yens instructing the children in self-defense techniques. By the end of the lesson each of the children had been thrown to the floor at least one hundred times and, despite the floor's sponginess, they were feeling bruised.

They slept soundly that night and awoke the next morning to find that they were both sore, but it wasn't a painful sore and they didn't let it stop them. Instead, they went straight out to the stables to spend an hour or so with Ed and Credalis before being summoned by Yens to the same room where the defensive training continued. By lunchtime, Aimee and Rodney were doing a lot more throwing and were being thrown a lot less, and Yens was pleased with the progress they were making. By dinner the children were very skilled at the techniques Yens was teaching, and he decided they were ready for the final phase of their training: weapons.

* * *

The next morning they reconvened in the room where they had been given their self-defense lessons. "What you see here," Yens said, opening his arms wide to indicate the mountings on the wall, "is a representation of every weapon ever used on Daak. Choose."

"Choose what?" the children wanted to know.

"You're weapon, of course. Choose a weapon that you will be comfortable with, one that you may become proficient at. Your weapon will become your best friend and may mean the difference between arriving in Frieer alive and not surviving the trip. Take your time and choose wisely."

Rodney had no trouble deciding on which one to pick. During breaks from self-defense training he had looked over the displays and identified a Truculan bow from the pictures in his book. He went to it now. Snatching it quickly from the wall, he held it first in his right hand and then in his left, enjoying the feeling of power it gave him. Extending his left arm he drew the string back with his right and discovered that it was adjusted perfectly for his size and strength. Removing the accompanying quiver and arrows from the wall, he returned to where Yens was standing and together they waited for Aimee to make her choice.

Aimee took her time. She strolled up one side of the room and down the other, inspecting the weapons carefully. The first thing to catch her eye was a long sword studded with jewels. But when she took it off the wall she found it too heavy to handle and had to struggle with both hands just to secure it back on its mountings. Eventually she, too, selected a bow and arrow set, though hers was very different from her brother's. Where Rodney's was a longbow, the kind that Robin Hood used to carry with one handle and one string, Aimee's was a compound bow. That is, it had several strings criss-crossing to provide extra stability. After playing with it for a little while to make sure that it was comfortable, she carried it over to where Yens and Rodney were waiting.

The twins were anxious to try their new bows out, but Yens was in no hurry to take them out to the target range. "As you have chosen, now shall you learn," he told them as he lowered himself to the floor. The children did the same as he continued. "I have told you that these weapons must become your best friends, but that cannot happen until you know what they are and where they have come from."

"I know where mine came from," Rodney said proudly. "It's a Truculan longbow, just like the ones that warriors and conquerors carry."

Yens nodded his head. "Very good, boy, but there is far more to the story than that. This very bow belonged to Fortis himself, the first and youngest king to ever rule over the Truculans. Though his reign was short, it was he who united the various Truculan tribes and lifted them from barbarism to civilization. Without Fortis, the Empire would never have existed. It is said that, after building the Truculan Empire, his job was finished and he simply faded away into history. Little is known about the young king, and legend has no doubt distorted some of the basic truths, but he did disappear suddenly and under mysterious circumstances. There are those who believe that he will someday return to restore the Truculan Empire to its former glory."

Rodney was very impressed by all this, and his face was beaming as he cradled the longbow.

"What about mine?" Aimee asked, lifting hers.

Yens took it from her and turned it over in his hands, looking at it very carefully before answering. "Foran village is but a small part of a larger kingdom called Atalan. The majority of the kingdom has already been captured by Haeron and is a miserable place to live, but it was once one of the most wonderful places on all of Daak. Years ago, when

Atalan wasn't nearly as developed as it is today, there lived a beautiful young maiden named Airia.

"Airia lived with her mother in a cabin set way back in the woods, so far back that, with the exception of a hermit who lived in a nearby cave, they were miles away from their nearest neighbor. Airia spent her days playing in the woods and hunting with a special kind of bow that she had invented to provide for her mother and herself. This is a facsimile of the one she had invented and is called an Airian bow in her honor."

"What is a facsimile?" Rodney wanted to know.

"A facsimile is a copy," Yens explained. "Unlike yours, this is not the actual bow carried by Airia, but it is one just like it. Anyway, by the time she turned eighteen Airia was perhaps the greatest marksperson in all of Daak, certainly the greatest that Atalan had ever produced. One day, some travelers happened to come upon Airia's cabin on their way to the king's castle. As it was late and they were tired, they asked if they could pass the night. Airia and her mother, whose name was Islana, were happy to accommodate them. They didn't have enough in their cupboards to feed the travelers, so Airia went out and killed a boar. She then brought it back to the cabin where she prepared it. That night they feasted, and when the travelers left in the morning they were well rested and happy.

"From there they went straight on to the castle, and when they arrived they told the king about the wonderful hospitality they had received from one of his subjects. They bragged about Airia's beauty and her skill with the bow. Now, the king was a very lonely man, and after his guests had left he decided to pay Airia a visit. Posing as a beggar, he arrived at the cabin and was offered food and lodging for the night. By morning he had fallen in love with Airia and, revealing his true identity, asked her to be his queen. Airia was quite flattered, as you can well imagine, but she had no desire to leave her mother or the woods that she loved so much, and she refused his offer.

"The king returned to his castle heartbroken and for months did nothing but mope around. Eventually, his depression became so bad that the entire kingdom began to suffer. The king's chief advisor, an old magician named Minoan, realized that something had to be done, and quickly, before the kingdom fell entirely apart. In the dead of the night he snuck out of the castle and approached the cabin where Airia and Islana were sleeping. Using a very powerful spell, he enchanted one of the young girl's arrows and then returned to the castle.

"The next day, the magician went to the king's chambers. 'Time to arise, Sire,' he said as he drew open the curtains. 'It is a beautiful day outside, and it would be a shame to waste it away in bed.'

"'Nothing can compare to the beauty of Airia,' the king replied. 'If I can't have her, then that is what I desire. Nothing.'

"'If that be the case then arise,' Minoan declared. 'Go now to the side of the fair Airia for tragedy has befallen her and she is in need of your comfort and compassion. Where she has spurned you before, now she will surely embrace your affections.'

"The king looked up with interest but was still doubtful because Airia's earlier refusal had been so definite. 'Are you sure?' he asked.

"'Have you ever doubted my counsel before?' the magician responded. 'Have I even once given you bad advice?'

"The king had to admit that Minoan had always guided him well, and for the first time in weeks he got dressed and faced his court. After taking care of some pressing business (which had been sorely neglected for quite a while), he called for his royal mount and rode off for Airia's cabin.

"When he arrived he found his beloved crumpled up on the ground, crying intensely. Dismounting, he hurried to her side and asked her what was wrong. She told him that she had gone out in the early morning to hunt and had waited patiently for hours without seeing anything. Then, suddenly, the largest stag she had ever laid eyes on broke into the clearing she was in. Moving slowly, so as not to startle it, she nocked an arrow and drew the string back on her bow. Taking her time, she set the shot up and only released the string when she knew her aim to be true. But instead of dropping the stag her arrow flew over its head and soared through the trees like it had a mind of its own. Frightened, she ran home as fast as she could only to find that the arrow had continued on its course until it had embedded itself in Islana's chest, striking her dead.

"It hurt the king to see Airia as grief stricken as she was, and he did everything he could to comfort her. He helped her to give Islana a proper burial, and then he sat up with her until she cried herself to sleep. The next morning the king made preparations to return to his castle. Before leaving he renewed his offer to take Airia with him and make her his queen. This time she accepted. She knew that if she were to remain in the cabin she would be constantly reminded of her mother's death.

"Airia married the king and eventually grew to love him as he loved her. She bore him several children, and as queen her every whim was taken care of. Eventually, she became happy again, but she never stopped missing her mother. For years she refused to touch her bow again, but she longed for the hunt and, despite the fact that it was considered undignified for a queen to participate in such activities, she spent time in the woods whenever she got the chance.

"It came to pass that, while stalking game during one of her trips into the woods, Airia encountered the hermit who lived in the cave not far from where her cabin was. She was happy to see him, for it had been a long time since their last meeting, but he did not seem to share her joy. When pressed for the reason that he was so solemn, he finally admitted that he had been carrying around a terrible secret. He had been out roaming on the night Minoan had visited the cabin, and he had seen the magician enchant the arrow that killed Islana.

"Realizing that her mother's death was not the accident she had for years believed it to be but an act of deliberate murder, Airia became outraged. She hurried back to the castle and confronted Minoan in his study, forcing him at arrow point to admit the truth. She wanted revenge and, in her anger, she let the arrow fly. Minoan acted quickly and used his magic to deflect the missile. Neither of them had anticipated that the king would walk into the room right at that moment, but he did and the deflected arrow hit him in the heart. It killed him instantly.

"When this happened, Minoan fled the castle and was never heard from again. Many people believe that Haeron is his great great granddaughter, but nobody knows for sure.

"In any case, the commotion alerted the castle guards and when they arrived they found Airia still holding on to her bow with her arrow embedded deeply in the king's chest. A summary trial was held and she was found guilty of treason and murder. As their eldest child was still too young to ascend to the throne and preside over the court, the lord chamberlain took it upon himself to pronounce sentence, and the sentence was death. Airia was hung in the castle commons and her body was buried without ceremony in a criminal's graveyard."

Both children were quiet for some time after Yens finished the story. Finally, her eyes full of tears waiting to spill, Aimee asked the question on both their minds. "Why did they hang Airia? Wasn't it Minoan who was responsible for both deaths?"

"Yes, but at the time the evidence seemed to indicate otherwise. The truth wasn't learned until Minoan's abandoned journals were discovered in a cave several years later, but by then it was too late. Airia's body, or what was left of it, was removed from the criminals graveyard and reburied with her husband's in the royal cemetery, but the truth couldn't restore her to life."

As Aimee thought this over, Rodney added his input into the conversation. But instead of his mouth, it was his stomach that spoke for him, filling the air with a loud rumble. The noise was a welcome relief to the sadness of Airia's tale, and while Rodney's face grew red with embarrassment, Aimee and Yens had a good laugh.

"Rodney's belly must be telling us it's lunch time," Yens said, still chuckling. "I have business to attend to, but Ho-Don will see to your needs."

CHAPTER SIX
The Crystal

For two days the children did nothing but practice with their bows. Aimee got the hang of hers first, but by the end of the second day the children were about equally as good and Yens was quite pleased with their progress. The decision was made. They were ready to leave for Frieer.

On the evening of their last full day in Foran village, the twins were escorted into the dining room for dinner. It was a quiet affair, much more civilized than mealtime usually was at Yenspetsnicksnack manor. Everyone was preoccupied with thoughts of the following day and Aimee would later liken the meal to prisoners eating their last supper.

As soon as dinner was over, Ho-Don brought the twins up to their rooms and locked them in while Yens excused himself to attend to business. He was never very specific about what his business was, and when asked by Aimee or Rodney he always responded as vaguely as possible, telling them it had to do with dealings he had to take care of as mayor and that they were too young to understand. The truth of the matter was that the twins would have understood perfectly well what he was up to. He just didn't want them to know.

Yenspetsnicksnack had not been completely honest with the children. There were some very important details he'd left out when he explained to them why and how he had brought them to Daak. He told them that Haeron had conquered most of the planet, and this was quite true. He told them that the majority of Atalan was under her domain. This was also true. He told them that Foran village was in the part of the kingdom that was still free. This was a lie.

Foran was one of the first villages to fall, and it had been directly under Haeron's power for many years. Her first act once she had conquered the village was to install a mayor who was loyal to her. A mayor who, by his betrayal of his own people, made it possible for Haeron to conquer the village in the first place. Yens was that mayor.

Haeron required that all of her mayors, regional governors and other appointed officials report in to her once a month. Because Yens was on an important mission, though, he was ordered to report in more frequently.

Even though the sorceress was a very powerful and very hateful magician, and while the majority of her magic was used for evil purposes, some of it did have practical applications. An example of this was the Crystal, a neat little device that allowed two-way communication between its owner and Haeron at all times. Through it, she disseminated all of her orders and monitored her domain.

Yens sat in front of the Crystal and pushed the one button that was set into the device below the glass orb. Lights began to flicker inside the glass and where mere moments ago nothing had been, there now existed the image of the evil sorceress. Yens knew that his likeness was at the same time being projected onto a similar device in Haeron's castle.

Despite what her name and reputation might suggest, the evil sorceress was beautiful. More beautiful than anyone had a right to be. If you knew nothing of her except her image, you would never expect that such a lovely body could house such evil. She had a slim, attractive figure, a face that could only be described as heavenly (despite the fact that it never smiled) and hair the color of the sunset. She employed or, more accurately, enslaved the finest tailors on all of Daak. Her clothing, therefore, was always of the highest quality and complemented her perfectly. She was, in all respects, a vision of loveliness.

Her personality, however, was as ugly as her outward trappings were beautiful, and this ugliness was mirrored in her voice. "This better be good news," her image snapped the moment it appeared. "I had to break away from a very enjoyable torture to answer your call."

Yens' voice, in contrast, was as sticky and as sweet as honey. "Everything is proceeding as planned, my liege. The children don't suspect a thing. They have accepted all of my lies without questions and think they're working against you instead of for you. They will go with me to enlist the help of Archimagus and the Hidden People, and when I discover exactly where the Secret City of the Hidden People is, I will report its location back to you so that your armies may attack."

Haeron looked thoughtful for a moment before replying. "Are you sure this will work, toad? I've sent some of my best scouts to Frieer and they were unable to locate the Secret City. Why should these children succeed where my own people have repeatedly failed?"

Yens had explained why to her several times in the past already, but because she could order his death at any time if she were in the least bit dissatisfied, he had to explain it again as diplomatically as possible. "This world was created through Rodney, my liege, and because of that he wields more power here than even he suspects. I understand the scope of his power and so will Archimagus. Where Archimagus has no reason to reveal himself to me or any of your other agents, he will look upon the boy as a powerful ally and contact him. When he does, I'll slap the manacles you gave me on him. If they work as you say they will…"

"Do you doubt me, maggot?" Haeron screeched. Blood flowed to her face and she thrust a crooked finger accusingly in Yens' direction.

Yens trembled and bowed his head low. "Of course not, Mistress. *When* the manacles work, Archimagus will be powerless, unable to work his magics. I will then deliver him unto you, and there will be no one on all of Daak left to challenge your supremacy. Prophesy shall not come to pass and your rein will have no end."

"When will you be ready to leave?"

"On the morrow. The children are sleeping now and we should be ready to go as soon as day breaks. And if you could be so merciful to arrange it so we are unmolested by your troops we should arrive in Frieer within a week. We'll have no problem meeting your Mid-Summer's feast deadline."

"Excellent. I shall issue the order to all my armies that you and your party shall be allowed to pass freely through their territories, but beware. Once you have reached the borders of the Dismal Forest you are on your own. The people of the forest are unknown to me and not yet within my dominion. I have sent many troops into the forest, but few have returned. I will not be able to assist you should you run into trouble there or beyond. And take heed when you reach the great Barrier Mountains. I have received reports of increased Wild One activity in that area."

Yens shuddered again. The Wild Ones were a savage, warrior people that existed only to kill. An encounter with them could very well mean the end of the mission and even worse the deaths of them all. "I understand, Mistress, and will take every precaution possible."

"Will there be anything else that you require?"

"No, my liege."

Haeron clasped her hands, interlocking the fingers. "You have done well, Yenspetsnicksnack, and shall be richly rewarded. When the head of Archimagus hangs on my scepter, you shall be named governor of all Atalan."

"Your majesty does me honor," Yens said, faking humility

CHAPTER SEVEN
The Ward

Training was over and they were ready to begin their journey. They started out bright and early the next morning. Actually, it wasn't very bright when they started out, but it was early. Yens led the way, followed by Rodney on Credalis and Aimee on Ed. Ho-Don rode in the rear with the packhorses.

The first day went well, but Yens had to continually remind the twins not to run their mounts. "Both you and your horses will need all your strength soon," he warned. "If you keep on like this we'll never make it half the distance."

At the end of the first day the children were so tired that they went right to sleep.

The second and third days were also uneventful, if a little quieter. Haeron had kept her promise to Yens and warned her troops away from them so they were able to travel without any kind of resistance. Although they had spent hours in the saddle practicing horseback riding, Aimee and Rodney weren't prepared for the long, ponderous pace of the horses and their rear ends became extremely sore. They continued on despite the pain, and by lunchtime of the third day the open fields and lightly populated areas they had been riding through gave way to rougher, more desolate territory. Just before dusk they found themselves facing a thick wall of trees.

"The Dismal Forest," Yens said as he halted the group. "Very mysterious and very dark. I don't know what dangers might lie ahead, so it's best we camp here for the night and enter it tomorrow when we're fresh."

The four dismounted and began to set up camp. The shelters went up more quickly than they had the previous nights, and it was barely dark before they were sitting around the campfire eating the simple but tasty dinner prepared by Ho-Don. Yens had stories he wanted to tell about the forest, but the children were too tired to listen. As soon as they had eaten, they turned in for the night and soon were both fast asleep.

Shortly before dawn Rodney awoke. Even though he had eaten more supper than Aimee and Ho-Don combined, he was hungry again. Climbing out of his small tent, he looked up at the sky. It was beautiful. The stars twinkled more brightly than they did back home because there was no pollution to dilute their glow. Crickets chirped loudly everywhere around him while a small brook gurgled away in the distance. He focused his attention on one of Ho-Don's packhorses and headed for it. Digging through the bag that the meal supplies were in, he made himself a pre-breakfast snack.

Momentarily satisfied, he looked around. Everyone else was still asleep, but they would be up soon so there was no point in going back to bed. A faint light was starting to leak through in the direction that the sun would rise in (his science teacher called it the crepuscular light) and it would soon be dawn. Not wanting to wake the others just yet, he decided to go for a walk.

As dim as it was, there was just enough light for him to see where he was stepping, and he headed in the direction of the stream. He stumbled twice in the semi-darkness but otherwise made it there unscathed. Bending over, he cupped his hands to catch the water and took a long drink. The water was ice cold but refreshing and he was absorbed in his own thoughts as he sipped it, completely unaware that he wasn't alone.

"Hi," someone said.

The word was spoken in a soft, friendly voice, but it was so unexpected that Rodney jumped up, spun around, and fell into the brook with a loud splash.

"Ugh," he grunted, shivering as the cold water swept over him. He stumbled as he stood back up, tripping once over a rock on the creek's bed, and then hopping back onto the shore. Assuming the battle stance that Yens had taught him during training, Rodney faced the intruder. "Keep back," he said, doing his best to force the fear from his voice. "I know how to fight like a Truculan and, besides, my friends are right over there. If I call out to them they'll be here in a second."

The stranger looked to where Rodney was pointing. Aimee, Yens and Ho-Don were still sleeping peacefully in the distance. When he looked back it was as if he was seeing Rodney for the first time. "Hi," he said again. "My name's Ward. Pleased to meetcha."

The stranger grinned and stuck out his hand. Rodney looked him over. He was about the same height and size as Rodney, and seemed to be roughly the same age. His hair was messed up and his clothes were dirty. It looked like he hadn't had a bath in over a week. He just stood there grinning from ear to ear with his hand stuck out, waiting for Rodney to shake it. Something about him looked familiar, and Rodney racked his brain to figure out what. Of course! He was the boy from the playground that had lost his ball. Relaxing, Rodney stepped out of the brook and shook the boy's hand.

"Hi Ward, I'm Rodney. We've seen each other before. You were playing in Foran Village about a week ago, when I first came to Daak. My sister Aimee still has the ball that you lost."

"No, that wasn't me," he said, breaking off the handshake but still smiling intensely. "I haven't been to Foran for a long time. I'm just coming from, hmm, I just came from, uh, actually I'm not sure where I just was, but I'm pretty sure that I haven't been to Foran since, ummm, well, for quite a while, I guess. That must have been Ward that you saw there."

A puzzled look formed on Rodney's face. "Wait a minute. Didn't you just say that your name was Ward?"

The boy smiled even brighter (if such a thing were possible) and stuck out his hand again. "That's right," he agreed. "My name *is* Ward. Pleased to meetcha."

Rodney suppressed a giggle as he shook the boy's hand again. "If you are Ward, and Ward was in Foran last week, then you must have been in Foran last week."

"That makes sense," Ward admitted, nodding in agreement, "so I guess we met in Foran. But since I haven't been to Foran for a long time, I don't see how we could have. I'm sorry, but I think you've gotten me a little confused." His forehead wrinkled as he considered what he had just said, but the smile didn't fade in the slightest.

Rodney shrugged his shoulders. "I think you're getting me confused, too."

"I know!" Ward shouted. "It must have been Ward that you met in Foran."

Ward seemed happy with this explanation, but it didn't do anything to clear up Rodney's confusion. "I think we're going in circles," he said, slowly piecing things together. "Do you mean that there's someone else named Ward who looks just like you and that he was the one that I saw in Foran the other day?"

Ward reflected on this. "Yes," he agreed, and it looked like it was the first time he had ever come up with the concept. "We are all named Ward. We're a, uh, um, a race. That's it, we're a race. And we're all named Ward. In fact, our entire race is also called Ward."

A little of the confusion lifted from Rodney's face. Ward's smile had a way of wearing off on others. "You mean that your name is Ward and you are a Ward at the same time, and everyone else who is a Ward is also called Ward?"

"Gee, you're smart," he said happily. "People usually don't understand Wards very well."

"I'm still not sure that I do either. What happens if two of you meet? I mean, you'd both be Ward then. What do you do?"

Ward wrinkled his forehead again. "I never really thought of that. Ward and I went swimming yesterday, and the day before Ward, Ward, Ward, Ward, Ward, Ward, Ward and me got together for a game of capture the flag, so I guess we must have had problems, but I don't remember any. I'll have to ask Ward."

"Anyway," Rodney began, his brain starting to hurt from all this. "What are you doing out here in the middle of nowhere?"

"Actually, I'm, umm, I'm not quite sure."

"Shouldn't you be at home right now?"

Ward looked up at the trees and then across the brook. "I am home."

"You mean you live here?"

"I play here."

Rodney took a deep breath and rephrased the question. "Shouldn't you be where your house is? I mean, aren't your parents worried about you wandering around like this so early in the morning?"

"Not at all," Ward answered. "In fact, I haven't seen my parents since my twentieth birthday."

Rodney took a step backwards and looked him over carefully. "What do you mean your twentieth birthday? You don't look any older than me, and I'm only twelve."

"Oh that," he laughed quietly. "All Wards look like me, except for the babies."

"Do you mean that you always look the same, even when you're old?"

"That's right. You're pretty smart, Rodney."

"How old are you, anyway?"

"Now let's see," he said, using his fingers to count with. "I'm pretty sure that I was with my parents when I was twenty, and then when I turned thirteen I went to the Wendleson's. I stayed there for quite a while, until I was thirty-five at least, leaving just before my twenty-third birthday. That was the year I turned forty, I think, so I…" he looked up and let his hands fall to his sides as he proudly announced, "I'm not really sure how old I am."

"Now let me get this straight," Rodney began, shaking his head. "Your name is Ward and you are a Ward. You look exactly like all the other Wards, who are also all named Ward, and none of you get any older than you are now. You don't know what you're doing out here or why, and you don't know where you've just come from either."

"That's right, Rodney! You understand me better than anyone I've ever met. Except for Ward, of course."

Rodney felt like he had been sent back in time and put into one of those Abbott and Costello movies that his father liked to watch. "I'm not sure I understand anything at all," he admitted, "but I'd like to. Let's start again. What are you doing here in the middle of nowhere?"

Ward's smile lost a little of its vibrancy, but it never left his face. "I explained that very clearly, I think. Or maybe I didn't explain it at all. I forget which. What are *you* doing here, Rodney?"

He didn't know why he should trust the Ward, but he did. Besides, he figured, Ward probably wouldn't remember anything that was told to him for very long anyway, so there was no reason not to tell him the truth. Rodney told him the whole story, beginning with when he drew the picture of Yens that came to life and ending with an explanation of the quest they were on.

"That sounds like fun. Can I come along with you? I'm sure I can be of some help."

"Aren't you afraid of the Sorceress?"

"Wards aren't afraid of anything," he said, again wrinkling his eyebrows slightly. "And since I'm a Ward, I guess that I'm not afraid of anything either." His smile grew back to its former intensity. He was overjoyed to have used logic effectively.

"Yens, that's the guy who brought us here and is leading us, might not like it but as far as I'm concerned…"

"I was going for a walk," Ward interrupted him.

"What?"

"I was going for a walk," Ward repeated. "You asked me what I was doing here and I was going for a walk. Then I forgot how to get back to, um, uh, ummm, that's funny, I can't seem to remember where I was. But I know where I am. Right here."

The Ward's confusion made Rodney smile. "Come on," he said, "Let's go wake the others and tell them that you're coming with us.

* * *

The first rays of sunlight were beginning to warm them as they got back to the campsite, and Ho-Don was just rolling out of his shelter to fix breakfast. He watched in disbelief as Rodney and the Ward walked back into the camp, the latter's arm outstretched and pointed in his direction.

"Hi. My name's Ward. Pleased to meetcha."

"Where did you meet *him*?" Ho-Don demanded of Rodney while refusing to shake the Ward's hand. After a few moments Ward dropped his arm back down to his side, but his ever-present smile gave no indication that he was aware of Ho-Don's insult.

"I went for a walk and stopped for a drink of water from the stream and Ward was there," Rodney explained. "He had gone for a walk too and gotten lost. He's decided to join us. When's breakfast?"

"The master won't like this," Ho-Don said, ignoring the question.

"You're right, I don't like this," an angry voice said from behind them. Yens glared at the boys as he stepped out of his tent. "We have enough problems without having to drag an idiotic ward along. He'll be nothing but trouble. He was getting along fine before you found him and he'll be okay once we're gone. He's staying here."

Rodney looked Yens dead in the eye. "I don't care how much trouble he might be. Ward is my friend, and if he says that he wants to come with us he can. You told me when you brought me here that you can't save Daak without my help. Well, you're not going to get it unless you include Ward in our plans. If not, I'll find another way to get home."

"Be reasonable, Rodney. There is no other way home. You need me as much as I need you, and neither of us need him. We'll all be much better off if we leave the Ward here."

Rodney folded his arms. "If you don't let Ward go with us, then I'm not going any farther either."

"Rodney can be very stubborn when he wants to be," Aimee said, joining the conversation. She stretched her arms and let out an early morning yawn before continuing. "He once stayed in his room for three whole days when Mom and Dad wouldn't buy him an Xbox, and even when he did come down he moped around for another week before he would do anything. And that was during summer vacation. You may be able to talk him into going without his friend, but it will probably take you several days to do it. What's wrong with having another person ride with us anyway? Ho-Don has two packhorses. Ward can ride the one that Ho-Don doesn't."

Yens straightened his back and spoke slowly. "I keep forgetting that you and your brother are new to Daak and therefore aren't familiar with the variety of unusual creatures living here. This is no ordinary little boy. This is a Ward."

"You say that like it's a dirty word. Are you afraid that he might be a spy for the Sorceress?"

A smile tugged at the corners of Yens' mouth. "I'm sure that he's not a spy for Haeron or anyone else. Wards are the stupidest beings on the face of the planet. If we bring this moron along he'll get us into no end of trouble. I'm sorry, but it's simply out of the question."

"So what if he's not as smart as us?" Rodney questioned. "Mom and Dad always taught us not to pass judgment on other people. It's not Ward's fault if he isn't smart, and we shouldn't treat him badly because of it. I meant what I said, Yens. Either Ward comes with us, or I stay here."

Against his better judgment, Yens gave in. "If it means that much to you he can join us, but he'll be your responsibility. I have neither the time nor the patience to deal with him. I'm still in charge, but you will be the one who will have to make sure that he's where he's supposed to be, when he's supposed to be there, doing what he's supposed to be doing. And if he wanders off and gets himself lost again, we won't have the time to go looking for him. Understand?"

A smile as big as the Ward's grew on Rodney's face and he nodded.

"Good. Now we've lost enough time this morning. Let's eat our breakfast and saddle up. I want to get through the Dismal Forest before the sun sets again if at all possible. Few people have ever spent a night inside the forest and lived to tell about it.

CHAPTER EIGHT
Gillian

Despite Yens' fears, the Ward was hardly a liability. He couldn't be called an asset, but he wasn't a liability.

The trail that entered the Dismal Forest was dark, rocky and uneven. The upper branches of the forest's taller trees crisscrossed high above the road, blotting out the sun and giving everything an eerie, mysterious appearance. Because of this, the group slowed their pace considerably.

The road began to twist more and more as they penetrated farther into the forest, and soon it was impossible to know what lay more than one hundred or so feet ahead of them. Each turn held the potential for surprise and, as Yens continually warned them, for danger.

They continued on, the plant life above them becoming thicker, the air around them becoming cooler and darker. The horses were nervous and so were the riders. Only Ward showed no sign of fear.

As they approached a particularly sharp bend in the road the horses became more unsettled and the children especially had a difficult time keeping their mounts under control. They made the next turn and were forced to stop suddenly. A huge tree trunk had fallen onto the road and was completely blocking their path. Yens got down from his horse to look the situation over, and the others followed his lead.

"What do we do now?" Aimee asked as Rodney dug through his saddlebag for a sandwich he had saved from lunch. Ward, more interested in what Rodney was doing than in what the problem was, went straight to the boy's side. Rodney ripped the sandwich in two and the Ward eagerly accepted the other half.

Yens walked carefully along the side of the trunk, kicking it every few inches. "It's too high for the horses to jump over and too solid for us to cut through it. I don't think that we can go around it, either, because we'd never get the horses through the thick foliage. If we go back and try to circumvent the forest we'll lose at least a week's time, probably more. The Dismal Forest stretches for hundreds of miles in either direction."

Leaving his packhorse, Ho-Don walked to where Yens and Aimee were. Noticing that the supply bags were now unprotected, Rodney and Ward snuck over and began rifling through the food bag while the others discussed the next plan of action.

"Might I suggest that we camp here for the night and think our options through, Master?" Ho-Don offered. "The sun is almost down anyway, and we can all use the rest and nourishment."

Yens frowned, but there really wasn't any choice. "Very well," he finally said, though he wasn't happy about it. "Let's get set up."

Ho-Don built a fire while Aimee and Yens started to put their tents together. As Aimee was stretching the strong fabric to where she had pounded her stakes in she came to a sudden realization: Rodney and Ward weren't anywhere in sight.

Aimee let go of her tent and stood up. The road where they were forced to stop was only wide enough for two horses to walk abreast. The thick forest walled them in on two sides and the fallen tree in front of them formed a third barrier.

"This isn't funny, Rodney," she yelled at the top of her lungs. "Come out of hiding right now." She looked up, half expecting him to drop down from the trees the way he did when they were going to the Murillos' house back home, but he didn't. When she looked back down Yens was at her side.

"How long have they been missing?"

"I'm not sure," Aimee answered. She was becoming frightened and had to take a deep breath to calm herself down. "The last time I saw them was when we stopped, about fifteen minutes ago."

Yens ran his hand through his hair and mumbled a word that Aimee had heard her father use a couple of times when he was angry and thought she wasn't listening. "If they wandered into the woods we'll never find them and they'll never find their way back. I knew I was asking for trouble when I allowed that moronic Ward to come along with us."

"What are we going to do?"

"Maybe they're wandering on the path back the way we came," he said, but the doubt was evident in his voice. "I'll have Ho-Don take his horse and ride back to check."

The pair turned to look for Ho-Don. The fire that he had built was now blazing away, but the servant was nowhere to be seen.

Aimee started to shake. "Yens, I'm scared."

"I know, but you can't let your fear overcome you. I want you to walk slowly to your horse and get your bow and quiver. I'll get my staff."

Swallowing hard, Aimee did as she was told. She gently stroked Ed's mane as she approached. "Easy," she whispered, more to herself than to her horse. Reaching into the saddlebag, she pulled her bow out, withdrew her arrows and turned around. Her knees began to shake and she had to stifle a scream.

Yens was gone.

She was all alone.

Her first instinct was to run. She wanted to jump on Ed and spur him down the path as quickly as possible, getting as far away from the area as she could. But then she thought what that would mean, abandoning Rodney and the others. Instead, she slowly went from one horse to the next, checking to see if all the weapons were still there. They were. When she reached Credalis she petted him gently and took her brother's arrows from the bag to add to her own. Nocking one in her bow, she sat on the ground between her half-built shelter and the fire. Not knowing what else to do, she waited.

Despite her fear, despite the uncertainty of what would happen next, Aimee managed to fall asleep at some point during the night. When she awoke, the fire had dwindled to smoldering ashes. Morning had come, but the thick network of branches above blocked out most of the light.

Throughout her sleep she had maintained a tight grip on her bow, and the arrow was still in place and ready to be fired. Her first thought as she stood and looked about her was that maybe everything had been a dream and that everyone would be sleeping safely in their shelters, but a quick survey of the area proved otherwise. She was still alone.

She was also hungry. Ho-Don had disappeared before he could make dinner, which meant that she hadn't eaten since yesterday's lunch.

Using a stick to turn the embers over, Aimee added some dry kindling to relight the fire. Having done that, she picked through Ho-Don's bag and pulled out the makings for oatmeal and toast. Simple, but it would suffice. Before taking care of her own needs, though, she remembered the horses. It had been just as long since they had eaten and she was careful to provide for them first.

Then, looking around again to see if there were any new developments, she settled down next to the fire. Laying her bow down close by her side, she placed a pan with water in it on a hook suspended from a tripod that straddled the fire. Then, putting two pieces of bread on the grill, she began to make toast. The water in the pan slowly came to a boil and Aimee added the oatmeal mixture. The entire time she had the uneasy feeling that she was being watched.

When everything was cooked she sat back to enjoy her modest breakfast. It wasn't the best meal that she had ever had, but it would ease her hunger. And, she realized, she felt a certain amount of satisfaction at having prepared it herself.

"Sister, why do you eat that gruel when you could be eating a fresh breakfast? There is game everywhere in these woods."

The voice startled Aimee and caused her to spill the oatmeal. In a smooth, fluid-like motion that she had learned during her training with Yens, she scooped up her bow and stood to face the speaker. She found herself looking into the eyes of a young girl about her height and age who was also holding a bow.

"Who are you?"

"Forgive me, sister," the girl said, extending a hand. "My name is Gillian."

Aimee reached forward to shake Gillian's hand, but the other girl reached a little farther and clasped on to Aimee's wrist. She, in turn, gripped Gillian likewise, and then the two released their hold on each other. "I'm pleased to meet you," Aimee said, remembering her best manners. "My name is Aimee."

"If you still hunger, sister Aimee, I would be honored to have you dine with us." Gillian pointed to a small deer lying on the ground with an arrow in its chest. "I have just completed my trial of ascension. I am now bringing my kill back to share with the sisters of my tribe and we will feast to celebrate my success. There is always room for another."

Aimee looked at her oatmeal, which was seeping into the ground. "Thank you," she said politely. "I would like that. But I have to return here afterwards. My friends are missing and I must find them."

Gillian bent down and took hold of the rope that she was using to drag her deer and then walked toward the foliage. "My word is my bond, sister. After the feast my sisters and I will help you locate your missing friends."

Gillian and the deer disappeared into the dense woods, and Aimee stuck close to her side for fear of getting lost.

* * *

It was a short trek through the forest, barely half a mile, but the uneven terrain made it seem longer. When they finally reached the encampment, Aimee was all out of breath. Gillian, despite having dragged the deer the entire way, was barely winded.

Aimee looked about. The camp was more like a small village built in a large clearing. Up above, the sun's rays came shining through a hole in the forest ceiling and down below dozens of long, stretched wooden houses were scattered throughout the area. Hundreds of people were wandering around or working on various projects. Everything looked peaceful, but something was wrong. It took Aimee a couple of moments to pinpoint what. Even with all the people in sight, she could not see a single man. There were only women in the village. She asked Gillian why this was so.

The girl dragging the deer looked puzzled by the question. "Is it not the same way in your tribe?"

Aimee was uncertain how to answer, and chose instead to change the subject, at least for the moment. She pointed to a small contingent that was coming to meet them. "There are some people heading our way."

Gillian smiled and waved to the approaching women, at the same time whispering to Aimee. "This is an important occasion for me, my first solo hunt. I've been out in the forest all week and now I have returned with success. The elders are coming now to see how I have done. When I show them my kill they will set up a feast to celebrate and then I will be inducted into the warrior class."

"You have done well," one of the women said. She had an air of importance about her, and she squinted as she studied the small deer. "But the hunt was supposed to be on your own. How is it that you return in the company of another?"

"This is my friend Aimee," Gillian answered, "a sister from another tribe, separated from her companions. I encountered her only after I had dropped my quarry and was on my way back. I have invited her to my feast."

The woman who had spoken first now looked Aimee over carefully. "Curious," she said, as much to the other elders as to the two girls. "I know of no other tribe, yet you wield the bow of the Sisterhood. I am Queen Exara. Welcome, little sister."

Queen Exara stuck out her hand. Thinking back to the way Gillian had gripped her upper wrist when she had introduced herself back on the path, Aimee reached past the Queen's hand and did the same. "Pleased to meet you, your majesty."

Exara tilted her head before releasing the handhold. "You wield the bow *and* know the greeting of the Sisterhood. Truly curious. There is much you must tell us, little sister."

The Queen was full of questions, but Aimee was short on answers. Remembering Yens' warning that the dark sorceress had spies everywhere, she was careful to be as vague as possible. Fortunately, Gillian was bubbling with excitement and anxious to tell every detail of her hunt. She dominated the conversation as they walked to the center of the encampment, and Aimee would have found it difficult to say much even if she had wanted to. Instead, she listened to every word and at the same time studied the camp. She wanted to learn as much about these people as possible before being forced to talk.

They skirted around the center of the camp, passing a series of tables and benches, and stopped before the entrance to one of the wooden buildings. "We have a surprise for you, sister Gillian. While you were undergoing your initiation last night, several of your sisters were also out in the woods where they encountered and captured an enemy raiding party. During the feast the prisoners will be sacrificed in your honor."

Gillian could hardly contain her excitement as the door to the building was thrown open. Aimee, at the same time, was nursing a feeling of dread deep down in her stomach. She looked inside and her biggest fear was realized. She saw the enemies chained helplessly to the wall and recognized them immediately:

Rodney, Yens, Ward and Ho-Don.

CHAPTER NINE
The Sisterhood

Aimee was confused. She wanted to tell Exara that these were her friends, but she was afraid that if she did she would be thrown in chains as well and then wouldn't be of any help to them at all. She decided, then, to pretend that she didn't know the captives. At least for the moment. This would give her time to work out a plan of rescue, she reasoned, but Rodney quickly ruined that idea.

"Aimee," he blurted out for all to hear. He had more to say, but Ho-Don swung a leg over and kicked him before he could get anything else out.

"Mistress," Yens said, taking over. "Please be merciful and do not question our loyalty. It wasn't our fault that we left camp without your permission. We were forced against our will."

"What are you talking about?" Rodney tried to say, but he only got the first two words out before being kicked into silence again by Ho-Don.

"Yes, Mistress," Ho-Don said loudly, trying to draw attention to himself before Rodney's confusion could give Aimee away. "Please don't beat us. It wasn't our fault."

Maybe it was because he saw his friend get kicked twice for trying to talk or maybe he was just confused by the whole situation, but for some reason the Ward remained uncharacteristically silent throughout all of this.

Queen Exara looked from Aimee to the men and then back. "You know these prisoners, little sister?"

"Yes, your Majesty," Aimee admitted, at the same time silently praying that she understood what Yens and Ho-Don were hinting at. "These are my slaves. They have been very loyal to me and I couldn't understand why they abandoned me back on the path. Now I see what happened." She took a long breath before continuing. "May I be allowed to reclaim them?"

The Queen studies Aimee for several seconds, her battleship gray eyes refusing to betray what she was thinking. "Curious," she finally said. "Be aware, little sister, that this situation is highly unusual, but I will call the Council of Elders together to consider your request. In the meantime, you will be treated as our guest. Sister Gillian will see to your needs."

The muscles tightened in Gillian's neck when she heard the last command. "But my feast…"

"Will be postponed until the Council has reached a decision. We must also ponder whether or not you are entitled to this feast. The rite of ascension is a singular test. A sister undergoing the ritual is required to go into the forest alone, spend a week there alone and return with her kill alone. You came back to the tribe in the company of another. And not just any other, but with a sister who carries the bow of a full-fledged warrior. There is much for us to discuss."

"That's not fair," Gillian blurted out before being silenced by a wave of the Queen's hand.

"If further input is needed on your part you will be summoned by the Council for testimony. Until then, your only responsibility is to our guest." Without another word, Exara turned and exited the building.

"Come," Gillian said softly as she tried to fight the tears that were threatening to fall. "We must leave now as well."

"Can't I have a minute alone with my frie … with my servants?"

"To do so could anger Queen Exara. She has quite a temper. She also has the respect of the Council and they almost always accede to her wishes. We must both remain on her good side if we want the Council's decisions to go our way."

Aimee wasn't happy, but she understood the logic of this. With a nod she followed the other into the open air.

* * *

"So what do we do now?" Aimee asked as they walked away from where her brother and the others were helplessly chained.

Gillian shrugged her shoulders. "We wait. Do you want to see where my feast will be?" Her head drooped a little. "Where it might be," she corrected.

"Sure," Aimee agreed, forcing a smile.

As they walked, Aimee looked carefully about her. When she first passed through the village she had been overwhelmed by the novelty of it all and only made vague surface observations. Now she studied the village with the calculating eye of someone who knew she might eventually have to escape from it.

The encampment reminded her of the Native American villages of the northeast she had studied in school. The Cayugas, a member of the Iroquois Confederacy of Nations, had once lived in the area of New York State where Aimee had grown up, and her teacher had spent a lot of time talking about how the Iroquois had once lived.

Looking around, she could see the similarities between the village of the sisterhood and those of the Five Nations of the Iroquois. There was no wall of vertical logs surrounding the clearing, but then again the thickness of the forest fenced it in and defined its perimeters as well as any human-made barrier might.

The buildings were set up exactly like the Iroquois longhouses that she had studied. Using trees for support, all of the structures were similar in shape, stretching along the ground like small railroad tunnels with no mountain to bore through. They were covered thoroughly with bark, from the bottom to the top, with little gaps left in the upper-most part of the ceiling to allow smoke from fires built inside to escape. Every single structure looked identical to the others. There were no design innovations or markings of any kind to distinguish them. As she noted before, people worked on various projects throughout the clearing, but the only people she could see were women and girls. There wasn't a man or boy anywhere in sight.

Presently they came to the middle of the village and Aimee noticed an end to the similarities between it and that of the Iroquois. There was a large open area here roughly the size of a football field. They had passed the area quickly on the way to see the prisoners, but Aimee wasn't able to get a good look at it then. Now she paused and studied it completely.

The first thing to catch her attention was a small but very ornate wooden structure that was placed dead center in the area. Next to it was a large charred pit. Dozens of crude, backless benches circled the structure and the pit. There were also several tables scattered throughout the area, but unlike the benches and the structure they surrounded, the tables had a temporary look to them as if they could be taken up and put away at a moment's notice.

"This is where my feast will be. If the Queen lets me have it, that is."

"I'm sure she will," Aimee said, hoping to cheer her friend up. When Gillian didn't respond, she tried a different approach. She pointed at the wooden structure in an effort to change the subject. "What is that?"

"The Altar of Airia," Gillian answered in a puzzled voice. "Surely your tribe must have one as well."

Aimee startled at the mention of Airia. She thought back upon the story that Yens had told the children and then looked down at the bow dangling loosely in her left hand. Things were slowly starting to make sense to her. "Of course we do," she lied, looking back up at Gillian, "but not one as beautiful as yours. Tell me about it."

Gillian sat down on one of the benches and Aimee followed her lead. "I don't know what there is to tell," she said, raising an eyebrow. "Airia was tricked into killing her mother by a man and then she herself was unfairly killed through the treachery of men. We use the altar to sacrifice any men we capture in her honor, to make redemption for the injustices forced by men upon Airia and all women."

Aimee swallowed hard. "When you say sacrifice, do you mean as in kill?"

Gillian raised her eyebrow again. "Doesn't your tribe kill the men it captures in the name of Airia?"

"No," Aimee said, remembering how Yens and Ho-Don addressed her in front of the queen. "We, um, we enslave the men we capture and force them to do our work for us. This, uh, it gives us more time to hunt like Airia used to do."

"It still seems easier to kill them," Gillian said simply. "There is plenty of time to hunt when work is finished."

Aimee stared at the altar and digested all this. "If the elders turn me down, will there be any way to prevent my slaves from being sacrificed?"

"None that I know of. Only in death may a man be of any use."

Aimee took a deep breath to fight back the tears that were threatening to spill from her eyes. “We can’t let that happen, Gillian. You have to help me come up with a plan to rescue them, just in case.”

“But why, sister? They are only men. Surely you can capture new slaves if Queen Exara decides that these ones must be sacrificed to Airia.”

“These are special slaves. I’ve had them for years and I’ve grown fond of them. They can’t be replaced. Please, Gillian, you have to help me.”

“I can’t. To do so would be to betray the Sisterhood and all that I believe in.”

Aimee was ready to argue, but before she could say anything she was distracted by a figure sprinting in their direction. The runner was a girl just slightly younger than Gillian and Aimee, and as she neared it became obvious that she was heading directly for them. Slowing up, she came to a stop in front of Gillian and the two girls greeted each other with the Sisterhood’s around-the-forearm handshake.

“Sister Gillian. I bring news from the Council of Elders,” the newcomer said clearly. Despite the run, there was no hint of her being even the slightest bit winded. “They wish to speak to you and the sister from the other tribe immediately.”

“Have they made their judgment, Kima?”

“I only know what I have spoken. But if they have, may judgment be favorable to you both.” With a nod, Kima turned and ran back from where she had come.

Gillian took a deep breath as Kima disappeared from sight. “It is time,” she said as she started walking. “Are you nervous, Sister?”

“A little,” Aimee admitted. “More afraid than anything else. I don’t know what I’ll do if they decide they’re going to kill my slaves.”

Gillian shrugged her shoulders. “As Airia herself once said, it’s pointless to worry about problems that may not exist. I have a good feeling about this, sister. Everything is going to work out for the best.”

* * *

Like all the other longhouses, the meetinghouse had no identifying marks of any kind to differentiate it from its neighbors. If she had been forced to find it on her own, Aimee wouldn’t have had a clue as to which building to go to. Gillian, however, having grown up in the village, was able to find it directly. The two girls paused in front of the doorway.

"What are we waiting for?" Aimee wanted to know. "Let's go in and find out what they've decided."

"The teachings of Airia remind us that patience is a virtue. We are not permitted to enter until an escort has been sent for us." Without another word, Gillian sat on the ground to wait and, having really no other choice, Aimee did the same.

Fortunately, the wait was not long. A member of the Queen's honor guard, a colorfully decorated young warrior in her mid twenties, came out to meet them and escorted them into the inner chamber of the Council of Elders. A large fire burned intensely on the chamber's dirt floor, the smoke swirling and reeling as it rose to escape through a hole cut in the tree-bark ceiling. The Queen sat cross-legged in front of the fire, and seven elders flanked her on either side, sitting around the perimeter so that they surrounded approximately three quarters of the blaze. The guard led the youngsters to a point directly opposite the Queen and then bowed respectfully before taking her place along the back wall with the rest of the honor guard.

Motioning with both of her hands, Exara bid them to sit down. They did as instructed and waiting for someone to tell them what to do. No one did. The Queen and all the elders looked intently at them, as if studying them, but no one spoke a word. Aimee was uncomfortable and she could tell by looking at Gillian that her friend was just as uneasy. Finally, after several minutes of this staring back and forth, Aimee decided to take the initiative and break the silence. "Has your majesty reached a decision on the fate of my slaves?"

The Counselors began muttering amongst themselves, quietly enough that neither girl could make out what they were saying. The Queen, meanwhile, continued to stare at the pair. Eventually, the talking between the Counselors ceased, and they directed their attention back to the two girls. Aimee felt more uncomfortable than ever.

"I will excuse this breach of protocol because you are a guest, sister, but know this: I am in charge here, not you. This is our chamber and I will do the talking. You will listen. The Elders and I have reached a decision, but we will attend to internal matters before addressing your outside concerns. Sister Gillian, rise."

Gillian was slow to move, and her legs shook as she stood up. Aimee could see that her friend was clearly intimidated by Exara.

Gillian lowered her head so that she was looking into the fire instead of past it. "Yes, my Queen."

"Sister Gillian. After much discussion, the Council is not convinced that you have successfully completed the Rite of Ascension. The title of Warrior is not given lightly. It must be earned. You returned to the Sisterhood in the company of another when you were instructed to complete the ritual alone. It is therefore our determination that you have not fulfilled the obligations of the Rite and will not be promoted to the Warrior class. Should you decide to do so, you may petition the Council again in two year's time for the opportunity to undergo the Rite of Ascension a second time. This petition may or may not be granted. Sit."

Gillian crumpled to the ground in a heap, tears spilling down the sides of her face. Aimee wanted to comfort her friend but was unable to because it was her turn to rise before the Council. Her stomach hurt and she shivered uncontrollably as she stood before Exara.

"Sister Aimee, your ways are new to us and we are trying to be tolerant of them, but we will not allow them to supersede our own. One of the primary beliefs of the Sisterhood is that all men are evil. The only way to purge their evil is to sacrifice them at the altar, sending their tainted souls to Airia for cleansing. We find it curious that you can become so attached to such worthless beings as men, but curious or not we cannot allow your slaves to continue. They will be executed at dawn. The Council has spoken. Our word is now law."

Aimee opened her mouth to protest, but before she could get anything out she was grabbed about each arm by a member of the honor guard and spun to face the door. Another pair of guards were pulling Gillian to her feet as well, and the two girls were firmly escorted to the outside.

Aimee looked at Gillian, not knowing what to say or even what to think. They stood there for several seconds before Gillian led Aimee away from the longhouse. Gillian brought Aimee to what could probably be best described as an alleyway between two other longhouses. She peered up and down the alley to make sure that they were completely alone before speaking. "I will help you to rescue your slaves, sister."

"But you said that would be betraying your tribe."

"True," Gillian said, her right eyebrow raised slightly. "But today my tribe has betrayed me."

CHAPTER TEN
Escape

The two girls discussed rescue plans and walked through the escape route several times as they waited for darkness to fall. When the sun finally set they were ready.

The Sisterhood of Airia was a tribe rich in tradition, and there were several rituals that were routinely observed. One of them was that all work stopped at sundown and a huge fire was built in the pit in the center of camp. A communal supper was cooked over the fire and all the sisters gathered together to eat and tell stories afterwards. The focus of tonight's stories would, no doubt, be the capture of the prisoners the night before and the meeting of the Council this afternoon.

Everyone was expected to attend this evening ritual, and all the guards charged with watching the captives, except for one, were temporarily excused from duty so that they could be there. Gillian and Aimee sat on stumps in the row closest to the fire so there could be no doubt that they were in attendance.

Dinner was excellent, a mixture of several different kinds of wild game alongside a strain of corn that Gillian explained was cultivated and harvested in a nearby clearing. When all the sisters had eaten their fill, Queen Exara stood alongside the Altar of Airia and addressed the throng. As was customary, she began by telling of the day's news, which in this case consisted of her relating the details of the meeting of the Council of Elders to the populace. There were several smaller domestic matters that were dealt with first, and then the Queen announced the decision that Gillian had failed the Rite of Ascension and would not be admitted into the warrior class. This was greeted with surprise and shock, and the Queen had to pause as the crowd talked excitedly amongst themselves.

Gillian held her head up high as her fellow sisters discussed her failure, despite the intense feeling of shame that was building in the pit of her stomach. She stared into the fire and tried to ignore the bits of conversation, mostly insulting, that filtered through to her ears. Whether her sisters admitted it or not, in her heart she was a warrior now and as one she was determined to not give them the satisfaction of seeing how much the decision had hurt her.

Eventually, all talk died down and the Queen continued, disclosing the fate of the captives. A wave of cheers and applause filled the air when it was announced that the prisoners would be sacrificed after all.

Aimee stood up amid all the clamor, tears cascading down her face as if a faucet had been opened wide in her eyes. Bumping into several sisters, she pushed her way out of the circle and fled crying into the night. As the crowd watched Aimee run, Gillian stood to face the Queen. "Please forgive her, Your Majesty. She doesn't understand our ways."

"Then go to her, sister," Exara responded in a voice both sympathetic and commanding. "Comfort her and help her to understand."

"Yes, my Queen." Gillian turned to follow in Aimee's wake.

"And Gillian," the Queen warned as the young girl approached the outer perimeter of the circle, "prevent her from doing anything foolish."

"Yes, my Queen."

* * *

Pausing to let her eyes adjust to the dark, Gillian focused on two longhouses lit dimly by the fire. She stepped out of the circle and headed for the gap between them where she found Aimee waiting just as they had planned.

"Did they buy it?"

"Buy it?" Gillian repeated, scratching her head.

"Buy it, you know. Did they take the bait? Did they believe it?"

"Oh," Gillian nodded, understanding. "They bought it better than I thought they would. You were great! I didn't even have to ask permission to go after you. Queen Exara ordered me to. Our absence is no longer suspicious because we have, what did you call it?"

"An alibi."

"Right. An alibi."

Aimee looked nervously about her. "What do we do now?"

"Right now there is only one warrior guarding the prisoners, so that makes this the best time to try and rescue them. But we must be careful not to harm the guard. She is still my sister, and where the Queen and the Council of Elders may have betrayed my trust, she has done nothing to hurt me. We'll need to somehow get the key away from her and keep her from alerting the others without doing her any permanent damage. It won't be easy. She is older and stronger than us."

"That may be true," Aimee conceded, "but surprise is on our side. I have an idea."

* * *

"I'm hungry," Rodney whined. He tugged at his chains for the thousandth time, but they still wouldn't budge. "When do we eat?"

"We fed you less than two hours ago," the lone guard answered.

"It feels like two forevers ago. I'm hungry again right now. Give me something to eat."

Without answering, the guard left, stepping outside to take a break from Rodney's constant complaining. That particular male seemed to be able to do only two things – eat, sleep and whine. She would be glad when her shift came to an end.

Pausing on the other side of the doorway she inhaled deeply, smelling the sweetness of the forest, feeling the cool air embrace her lungs. The corners of her lips curled up in acknowledgement of the pleasure the fresh air was giving her, but the smile quickly wiped itself from her face.

A sound from the darkness startled her, and she automatically tensed up. Squinting, her eyes locked on two forms heading in her direction. With a swift, fluid motion she plucked an arrow from her quiver and nocked it. She started to draw back on the string, but relaxed when a shaft of light from one of the moons revealed the identity of the approaching pair. "Sister Gillian," she nodded, placing the arrow back in her quiver.

"Sister Maltah," Gillian answered, greeting her with the forearm handshake.

Knowing the importance the tribe placed on tradition and ceremony, Aimee waited until they were done and then offered the guard the same greeting. "Sister Maltah."

"Little sister," Maltah responded. A look of confusion came over her face as they broke the embrace. "Why aren't the two of you at the fire?"

"Queen Exara has announced that the prisoners are to be executed," Gillian explained. "She has given sister Aimee permission to bid her slaves farewell before they are dispatched to Airia for cleansing. I was asked to accompany her.

"But why now? They won't be sacrificed until morning."

"Because I wanted a little privacy, sister," Aimee answered. "The Queen granted my request to visit them now while everyone is at the fire because it is the only time I'll be able to be alone with them."

Maltah thought this over. "This is very unusual, but if Exara has ordered it, so shall it be. But I'm afraid I cannot allow you to be completely alone with them. I must go with you."

Without another word, Aimee, Gillian and Maltah went inside. Aimee headed straight for Yens. "Have you been hurt in any way?"

"No Mistress," he answered. Looking at his hands he rattled the chains binding them. "My wrists are sore, though."

Aimee looked Yens dead in the eye. "At least they didn't chain your legs," she said, slowly and deliberately.

"Yes Mistress," Yens replied with a glimmer of understanding. The conversation continued with Maltah and Gillian leaning against the front wall looking on. After several minutes, Aimee clutched her side and dropped to her knees right in front of Yens.

"Mistress!" Yens shouted.

"My appendix," Aimee screamed. Her face twisted in agony. "I think it's ruptured. I need your help."

Without hesitation, Maltah ran to the little sister's aid. As soon as she came near, Aimee rolled out of the way just as Yens swung both legs up, gripping the chains with his hands to support his weight. His legs came back down, wrapping around Maltah's neck and drawing her to him. At the same time, Gillian raced over and grabbed Maltah's bow and keys. While Gillian released the prisoners in turn, Yens held the guard tight. He was the last to be unlocked, and as soon as he was free he slapped the chains on Maltah.

"I was hoping you would understand what we were doing when I made the comment about your legs being free."

Yens rubbed his wrists where the chains had been. "I wasn't completely sure at first, but I figured it out when you fell to the ground. Good thinking, Aimee."

"It's not that big a deal," Rodney stated. "They use that trick to get out of prisons on *Star Trek* all the time. I always knew Aimee secretly watched it when she pretended that she wasn't interested."

Aimee wanted to tell her brother to shut up, but she was distracted by the sounds of as scuffle near the back of the building. Ho-Don and Gillian were wrestling, rolling back and forth on the ground.

"Let her up," Aimee yelled. "She's helping us."

"You heard her," Yens snapped when Ho-Don did not immediately stop. "Let the girl up."

Reluctantly, Ho-Don stopped and stood up. Gillian also got to her feet, the two of them glaring at each other as they brushed themselves off.

"Traitor," Maltah spat from where she was chained.

Gillian looked down at the dirt floor. "I do what I must do," she said as she tossed the keys just out of Maltah's reach. "Someone will discover you soon, but by then we will be long gone."

"Don't be so sure," a voice said from the doorway. All eyes turned to look at Exara. The Queen held her bow in her hand, the drawstring pulled back. An arrow pointed in the general direction of the group was nocked and ready to fire. "I must admit that I am disappointed, Gillian, but not necessarily surprised. Release Maltah and chain the prisoners back up."

Gillian bent down and picked the keys back up. She made a pretense of unlocking Maltah, but at the last second flung the heavy set of keys at Exara, striking her in the head. The arrow shot from the bow, embedding harmlessly in the wall about six inches from Aimee. Taking his cue, Yens grabbed the dazed Queen and put her in chains right next to Maltah.

"We must move fast," Gillian said with urgency. "When Exara doesn't return the others will come looking to see what has delayed her."

"Too late," Rodney said from the doorway. "Here they come now." The entire tribe was approaching, some wielding torches, all carrying weapons.

"Then move it," Gillian ordered. She ran out the opposite door and the others followed. They paused at the edge of the forest. "Everyone hold hands. The thickness of the treetops will not permit moonlight to penetrate and we will be all but blind. Do not worry, though. I can get us to your horses. I have known these woods since I was a babe."

So have all your sisters, and they all have torches, Yens thought as he looked back at the approaching women, but he kept his thoughts to himself. They didn't stand much of a chance in the forest, but it was better than the chance they would have if they stayed where they were.

Moving was awkward. But somehow, even though they were forced to hold hands and couldn't see where they were going, they still made good time. Gillian led them, weaving around rocks and trees, over rises and through depressions. Still, the tribe was gaining and it became obvious to Gillian that her sisters would catch up to them before they could reach the horses if they continued on as they were.

"Over here," she said, dragging the others behind a large cluster of trees and bushes. "We're never going to get there first. Our best hope is to hide, let them pass, and hope they don't realize what we're doing."

Following Gillian's example, the group squeezed its way into the midst of the cluster, crouching as low as possible to avoid being spotted when the sisters and their torches went by.

"Don't make a move or a sound," Gillian warned as soon as they were all situated. "My sisters are hunters, trained to detect any movement. Be as still and as quiet as possible."

They didn't have long to wait before the tribeswomen reached them. Aimee felt every beat of her heart and had to fight the urge to scream as the light from the passing torches flickered in and out through the holes in their hiding place. One sister stopped right in front of them and looked the area over, but she continued on without incident. They waited there for several minutes after the last of their pursuers was gone.

"Good," Gillian finally said as she helped everyone out of hiding. "That worked, but we're still not safe. We must assume that they have anticipated our plan and will leave guards by your camp. Meanwhile they'll send out hunting parties back into the forest for us. We'll have to elude the parties before we can even think of how we're going to get past the guards."

Aimee gulped. "Do you have a plan?"

"Not even a clue."

"Let's get to the horses first," Yens decided. "We can figure out what our next move should be then."

"Your slave speaks wisely, sister," Gillian said. "We should heed his advice, even if it did come from the worthless mouth of a man."

They moved slower now, walking cautiously and stopping every few steps to look and listen for signs of ambush. Despite the odds, they made it to the horses safely. They crawled on their stomachs to the edge of the path and surveyed the situation through the cover of the forest. The sun was beginning to rise and, though the branches overhead were tightly packed together, enough light found its way through to allow them to see.

"This is impossible," Gillian whispered after she had scanned every inch of the area. "There's no indication that the Sisterhood has been here, yet they had to have known that this is where we were headed."

"It could be a trap," Aimee suggested.

"There's only one way to find out," the Ward smiled, his teeth sparkling in the early morning glow. Without another word he rose to his feet, stepped through the foliage and walked right up to the horses.

CHAPTER ELEVEN
The Barrier Mountains

The air was thick with tension as the Ward stepped into the open. Everyone watched intently, expecting the worse. Nothing happened. He circled the area, but still nothing. "There's no one here," he said with a grin.

Rodney exhaled with relief as he suddenly realized that he had been holding his breath. "It looks like we're safe," he whispered.

"Perhaps," Yens agreed, "or perhaps they are waiting until we are all exposed before they attack."

They sat and watched for several minutes more, scanning for any possible ambush sites. Ward grew tired of waiting for them and began digging through Ho-Don's saddlebags for food. He found a chunk of jerky and bit into it, savoring its taste.

Rodney drooled as he watched his friend eat. Enough was enough. Jumping up, he ran to the Ward's side and fished through the saddlebag for a piece of his own.

When they finished, they started searching for more to eat. It was at this point that Yens decided to come out of hiding. The danger of the trap still existed, but if he sat and watched for much longer there was the more immediate danger that Rodney and the Ward would eat all of their provisions. He stepped cautiously into the open and looked around carefully. When he was as satisfied as he could be that it was safe he called to the others to come out of hiding.

Everyone was nervous now that the entire group was completely exposed. It was the perfect time for the sisterhood to spring a trap, but still nothing happened. The forest was as still as ever. Yens turned and looked at Gillian.

"Unfortunately we are but simple travelers and have nothing with which we can repay you for what you have done. I can only offer you my thanks for your assistance. We would never have escaped without you."

Ignoring him, Gillian looked at Aimee. "There is but one way to repay me, sister. You must take me with you."

Aimee tried to speak, but before she could get a word out Yens responded. "I'm afraid that isn't possible. Our party is too large as it is and we don't have an extra horse to offer you. As much as we are in your debt for everything you have done, our paths must part here."

"You have to take me with you," Gillian pleaded, still directing her conversation to Aimee. "My sisters know it was I who helped release your servants. If I were to go back to my tribe now I would be executed as a traitor. I helped your servants avoid that fate, and now I ask you to return the favor for me. Surely the sisters in your tribe will offer me refuge when they learn what I have done for you."

"We can't let her be killed for helping us, Yens," Aimee said. "She can ride on my horse with me if necessary, but she has to go with us."

Recognizing that he had no choice, Yens gave in. "I suppose, but she'll have to do everything I tell her while we're underway."

Gillian straightened up and threw her shoulders back. "I take orders from no man," she proudly announced. "I will listen only to you, sister."

Yens winced and opened his mouth to speak, but Aimee silenced him with a wave of her hand. "It will be all right," she promised.

"Right now, though, I must insist that you all listen to me," Gillian added. "I do not know why my sisters did not come here directly to wait for us, Aimee, but this is the spot where they captured your servants. It won't be long before they realize that we have come here. We must leave as soon as possible."

"Agreed," Yens nodded before changing his tone of voice to that of an order. "I want everyone to mount up now. Time is of the essence."

"But our shelters," Rodney protested. "And Ho-Don's cooking stuff."

"You must leave them," Gillian answered for Yens. "Even now my sisters could only be seconds away. If they recapture you now there will be no chance for a second escape. We will all be killed immediately."

Yens swung himself onto his horse. "Do as she says," he commanded. "Let's get out of here."

"But what about the fallen trunk in front of our path?"

Yens shrugged. "We don't have time to find a way around now. Like it or not we'll have to go back the way we came. It will mean a delay, but at least we'll be alive to continue on with our mission."

"What trunk?" Gillian asked.

"Why, the..." Aimee's jaw dropped and the words stopped coming out. Shifting in her saddle, she lifted her right hand and pointed. "Look!"

"The log's gone," Rodney exclaimed. "How can that be?"

"I don't know," admitted Yens, "but I'll not worry about it now. Come on."

Yens spurred his mount on, forcing it to run as fast as it was able on the rocky and uneven path. Rodney was able to keep up with him on Credalis, and the extra weight didn't seem to slow Ed down any, but the packhorses carrying Ho-Don and the Ward were a bit slower. Yens ordered the twins to ease back on the reigns as he did the same himself, and they waited for the others to catch up to them. When Ward and Ho-Don had reached them they kept a slower pace by letting the packhorses take the lead. After about an hour Yens gave the order to drop the horses back down to a trot.

"They'll never catch us now," Yens explained when Rodney questioned the order. "Not as long as they remain on foot. And I saw no evidence of them having horses."

"We have none," Gillian admitted. "The forest is so thick in most places that we have found walking to be the most effective means. You are correct, slave, we should be safe now."

Rodney did what he was told and slowed down with the group, but he wasn't happy about it. "Why take any chances? The faster we move, the quicker we'll be out of this forest. Then we'll be safe for sure."

"There is logic to your words," Yens admitted, "but you have not taken all the factors into consideration. While our horses are well rested, they have neither eaten nor taken a drink for more than a day. We have to be careful not to overdo it, or we may end up driving them right into the ground. Instead we will advance slowly until we come to a suitable place to water them. There we will feed them and take on nourishment ourselves. We will then be in a much better position to continue on with our journey."

They rode at the more relaxed pace for most of the day before finding a place to stop. For the first few hours the landscape remained virtually unchanged. The twisting path was as full of rocks, holes and bumps as it had been since they entered the forest, and the trees continued to wall them in on both sides as well as from above.

Eventually, though, the plant life started to become less and less dense and the occasional ray of sunlight managed to sneak its way through the canopy of branches overhead. The path gradually became straight and even, and by early afternoon the Dismal Forest was little more than an open woodland. A small brook gurgled lazily alongside the path for a distance, and it was here that they stopped to water the horses and take a quick lunch.

With the horses taken care of they were able to move them a little faster. Traveling became easier as the forest continued to open up, and they made better time in the afternoon. Through the increasingly sparse trees the travelers were able to catch infrequent glimpses of a mountain, and in the distance they could hear a faint rumbling sound.

Presently they reached a point where the trees were thin enough and the ground high enough that they could see what was ahead of them, and Yens halted the group. "The great Barrier Mountains," he announced with pride as he waved to what lay before them.

"It's beautiful," Aimee said as she drank the landscape in.

Behind her, Gillian nodded in agreement. "I've never seen anything like this before in my life. So much open space."

Several gently rolling hills stood in formation, one behind the other, each covered with lush green grass and sprinkled with a colorful assortment of wild flowers. But it was the mountains beyond the hills that dominated the view. Parts of several were visible, but only the closest could be seen in its entirety. Still more than a mile ahead of them, it was so massive that the children felt they could almost reach out and touch it. It towered so far into the sky that its top was hidden in a bank of clouds, but it wasn't the top of the mountain that captured their attention.

About a third of the way up, an underground river broke through to the surface, pouring its waters over a ledge and down the side of the mountain. This was the rumbling sound that they had been hearing.

Hundreds of miniature rainbows danced in the suspended vapors of the mist formed by the impact of the water, growing and dissipating at will and casting an almost magical glow over the area. The children all stared, mesmerized by its beauty.

After a quick discussion, it was decided that they would head for the waterfall and begin their search for a way through the mountains there. The path that had led them through the Dismal Forest disappeared into the grassy terrain of the foothills right before them, but that didn't impede their progress. The mountain so dominated the landscape that they were always able to keep their destination in sight.

* * *

There were still a couple of hours of sunlight left when they reached the waterfall, but Yens decided that they had gone as far as they were going to go for the day. They would rest up from their escape, and in the morning they could look for a place to begin crossing the mountains. According to the map that Yens had taken from one of his books in the library, there was a pass nearby that would take them straight through the Barrier Mountains and into Frieer. They would find its entrance after breakfast and then begin the last leg of their journey.

After the decision to stop was made camp was set up by the small lake formed at the bottom of the waterfall, on the opposite side of the falls itself. Setting up the camp was easier this time than it had been on previous nights, because there was very little to do. Most of their equipment had been left behind during their escape from the Sisterhood of Airia. While Ho-Don tended to the animals and searched the area for suitable wood to build a fire, everyone else found themselves with some free time on their hands. Yens grabbed a long stick from the pile that Ho-Don had already collected and tied a string to it. At the other end of the string he attached a hook and then looked up at the children and the Ward who were watching him with interest.

"Why don't we go see if we can catch us something fresh to cook for dinner?" he said as he handed the makeshift fishing pole to Rodney. Then, after looking unfavorably at the grassy bank closest to them, Yens started to walk along the water's edge.

They moved in the direction of the mountain, with Ward and the twins following Yens, and Gillian following Aimee. They had to go quite a distance before the grass gave way to rocks, and it was where the rocks began that the group stopped. Turning one of the smaller stones over, Yens reached down and plucked a large yellow bug that was hiding underneath. "There," Yens said with a smile as he impaled the squirming creature on the end of Rodney's hook, "that should do it. Let's see what bites."

Rodney went to the shore and tossed the hook in. Every once in a while there would be a tug at the end of the line and the bug would be gone, but after baiting and losing several insects he had yet to catch a fish. Yens and the Ward took turns as well, but neither of the girls wanted anything to do with it. After watching for a little while with fading interest, Aimee decided that she would rather go for a swim.

"You can't" Rodney said when she voiced her desire. "You'll scare all the fish away."

Now, Aimee was happy with the way she had held up throughout their time on Daak, and extremely proud of the maturity she had shown in the camp of the Sisterhood, but she was, after all, still a twelve-year-old girl. She was tired and cranky, and the thought of her brother telling her what to do got her mad. "I can if I want to," she snapped, looking him dead in the eye. "And there's nothing you can do to stop me. Besides, there aren't any stupid fish in there or you would have caught one by now."

"Your brother's right," Yens said, trying to stop the fight before it got any worse. "We're having a tough time now as it is. We'll never catch anything if you girls start splashing around in the water."

"I don't care," Aimee answered. "Rodney's not the only member of our family who can be stubborn. I'm hot and I'm dirty. I haven't had a bath since we started this dumb journey and I'm going swimming whether you like it or not."

Yens took a deep breath and ran a hand through his hair. "Okay. If you want to go swimming then go swimming, but please do it somewhere else."

"Fine. I will," Aimee quipped. "Come on Gillian." Without another word the two girls stomped away, heading back along the edge of the water in the direction of the camp. The shoreline twisted ahead of them, bending around a small rise, and they didn't have to go far before they were out of sight of the others. Before them the lake opened up into a miniature bay with a small patch of golden sand between the water and the grass.

"This looks like the perfect place," Aimee said as she stripped to her underwear and gently folded her clothes on the edge of the sand. "Let's go in."

Aimee leaped over the tiny beach and touched the water with her toes. The temperature was comfortable enough, and she waded in to her waist before noticing that her new friend was still standing on the shore. "What's the matter?"

"I'm afraid," Gillian admitted. "We don't have anything like this in the forest. There was a stream near our village where we used to bathe, but it was not deep. I could always see the bottom. But here you've only taken a few steps and the level is already halfway to your head. What if it is deeper in places than we are tall? We will be killed."

Aimee thought this over for a second. "You mean you can't swim? No, of course not, there wasn't any place where you could learn. I tell you what, Gillian, walk where I walk and you'll be safe. I promise not to go any deeper than this."

Aimee's promise was good enough for Gillian, and with some hesitation the latter shucked her outer clothing and walked into the water. Whatever reservations she had quickly disappeared, and before long the two girls were laughing and splashing each other, becoming so absorbed in their games that they temporarily forgot the seriousness of the situation. After about forty-five minutes of playing, they raced back to the shore and dropped on the sand to let the sun dry them off.

"Can I ask you a question, sister?" Gillian said, slicking back her wet auburn hair.

Aimee pushed her own blonde hair out of her eyes and rolled onto her side. "Of course. We're friends, aren't we?"

"Yes we are, but there is something about you that bothers me. You are of the Sisterhood, yet you sometimes allow yourself to be ordered about by your slaves. It is very confusing."

"It's time I was honest with you. The people I'm traveling with aren't my slaves. I just said that so your sisters wouldn't put me in chains as well. Rodney is my brother and the others are my companions.

And I listen to Yens because even though he can be a real pain sometimes, he's the only one who can help me and Rodney get home. At least he says he is. There's something about him that I don't trust but Rodney does, and we really don't have any other options. Do you hate me for lying to you, Gillian?"

Small waves gently nudged the shore near their feet. "If you had told me the truth yesterday I would never have helped you escape and your friends would be dead now. You did what you had to do. But I don't know if I'll ever be able to think of a man as my equal, like you seem to. I will try to tolerate them out of respect for you, sister, but it won't be easy. I grew up believing that they are lesser beings worthy only of death, and I have yet to observe anything to shake that belief. But enough of that. Tell me why it is that you traveled through my forest and now seek to cross these mountains. I have been cast into your company. It is only fair that I know what that means."

Aimee was prepared to tell her all about the evil Sorceress and their quest for Archimagus and the Hidden People, but before she could begin she was interrupted by laughter only a few feet away from them.

"I see London, I see France. I see Aimee's underpants." Rodney's voice teased between giggles.

The girls looked up to see Rodney with his arms outstretched, still laughing as he held Gillian's outer clothing in his fingers. The Ward was standing there also, laughing even harder as he held Aimee's clothes in the same way.

"Give those back," Aimee demanded.

Rodney shook his head. "You gotta catch us first." Without another word, Rodney and the Ward began running.

Gillian was the first to her feet, and in less than a second she was running like a flash after them. With a leap that would put most cats to shame, she flung herself in Rodney's direction, grabbing him by the legs and bringing him to the ground. The impact knocked the breathe out of Rodney, and Ward stopped to watch in amazement as Gillian wrestled her clothes back with ease.

The Ward was so busy watching, in fact, that he failed to notice Aimee sneaking up on him. She grabbed his right arm from behind, twisting it and jamming it up his back, forcing him to his knees. "Say 'uncle'," she demanded.

He said it without hesitation and Aimee let go of his arm while quickly snatching her clothing back. At the same time Rodney rolled over onto his back and began to sit up. The two boys nursed their wounds as the girls put their outer clothes back on.

"That hurt." Rodney whined as he stood to massage his arm. "You didn't have to tackle me so hard."

"And you didn't have to steal our clothes in the first place, so I don't feel sorry for you," Aimee said, defending her friend.

"We were just playing."

"Well, it wasn't funny."

Knowing in his heart that his sister was right, Rodney decided not to continue the argument. He extended a hand to help the Ward back to his feet. "Are you all right?"

The Ward nodded, his smile already returning to his face. "I like being with you people. I haven't had this much fun since, well, since the last time I had this much fun, and I can't remember when that was. Can we do it again?"

"No!" Aimee and Gillian shouted in unison.

"Okay," responded the ever-agreeable Ward. "Let's play another game then."

"Why don't we go back to camp instead," Aimee suggested. "I don't know about anybody else, but I'm starving. Let's go see what Ho-Don has for us to eat."

Rodney stuffed his hands in his pockets. "Okay, but I bet it won't be fish. Yens still hadn't caught anything when we left to see what you guys were doing."

When you came to pick on us, Aimee wanted to say, but she thought better of it. There was no point in starting another argument. Instead, they walked silently in the direction of camp.

When they got there the place was deserted. "Ho-Don must still be out looking for wood and Yens must still be fishing," Aimee hypothesized.

"Then we have time for another game," Ward said excitedly.

Rodney nodded his head. “And I have just the game. It’s called food hunt.”

“That sounds like fun, Rodney. How do we play?”

“Simple. While Ho-Don is away, we go through his food bag and see what we can find. The object of the game is to find as much food as we can.”

“And then what?”

A smile grew on Rodney’s face big enough to rival that of the Ward’s. “And then we eat it. We’ll have to hurry, though. The sun will be going down soon, which means we won’t have a lot of time before Ho-Don and Yens get back to ruin the game.”

“That really sounds like fun, Rodney. Let’s get started.”

“I’ve got a better idea,” Aimee said as she fished into her jacket pocket. She pulled out the ball that one of the Wards had lost in Foran Village and tossed it into the air. “Why don’t we throw this around instead. Yens and Ho-Don will be back soon enough and then we can eat.”

“Okay, Aimee,” Ward agreed. “That sounds like fun too.”

“Hold on,” Gillian said as she looked to the horizon. “I do not wish to spoil your game, Sister, but I don’t think you’re going to get a chance to play. Here comes your slave Ho-Don now.”

Disappointed, Rodney lifted his head to see where Gillian was looking. “Why’s he running?”

“I don’t know,” Gillian admitted, “but he’s moving pretty fast. It looks like he’s yelling something, too, but I can’t make it out because the waterfall is too loud.”

“He keeps saying ‘mount up’,” Ward said matter-of-factly. “This is a fun game, too. Want me to yell and see if he can hear me?”

The twins looked at each other and then at Ward. “Are you sure that’s what he’s saying?”

Ward nodded, and the twins moved as one to unhitch the horses. The children were climbing onto their mounts as Ho-Don reached them, rocks whistling above his head.

“Wild Ones,” Ho-Don explained between breaths as he jumped on the nearest packhorse. He pointed toward a patch of trees back the way they had come. “This way. Maybe we can lose them in the woods.”

“But what about Yens?” Rodney asked. “He’s still fishing in the other direction.”

“The Wild Ones won’t take us prisoner and give us a chance to escape, boy,” Ho-Don shouted back. “They’ll kill us right on the spot. If Yens isn’t dead already he will be soon. We have to worry about ourselves. Now do what I say and head for the trees or we will all be joining him.”

“No,” Rodney screamed. Without waiting for Ho-Don to continue the argument, he spurred Credalis on in the direction where he had last seen Yens. “Not if there is a chance that he’s still alive.”

“Get back here or you’ll be killed,” Ho-Don yelled, but it was no use. Rodney had already made up his mind and there was no changing it.

CHAPTER TWELVE
The Wild Ones

"The fool," Ho-Don muttered to Aimee as he watched Rodney ride off. "He's as good as dead, but at least I still have you."

Aimee glanced at Ho-Don questioningly, but it was the Ward who made the next move. He jumped off the packhorse that he had been riding and climbed onto Yens' stallion. Jabbing it in the sides with his heels, he chased in Rodney's wake like an expert horseman.

Then, as Ho-Don looked on in disbelief, Aimee made up her mind. "Hold tight," she told Gillian as she followed the Ward's lead.

Left alone, Ho-Don hesitated as he looked one last time at the safety of the trees. Shaking his head, he prodded the packhorse he was sitting atop of in the direction the others had gone. The second packhorse, the one that Ward had abandoned, followed of her own accord.

* * *

The setting sun painted streaks of reds and yellows in the sky, streaks that reflected off the waters of the lake. Lost in thought, Yens studied the richness of the colors until a sharp tug on the end of his line snapped him back to reality. Pulling up on the makeshift pole, he set the hook and prepared to hoist his catch in. He never got the chance.

Something hit him sharply in the back of the head, driving him to his knees and forcing the stick from his hands. Reaching to where he had been struck, Yens felt something warm and sticky covering his fingers. Blood. He started to black out and had to struggle to maintain consciousness.

Gaining at least partial control of his sensibilities, Yens hugged the ground, trying to keep as low as possible. Lifting his head just enough to see, he scanned the surrounding areas looking for cover, knowing that he had to get to some kind of safety before another projectile could strike him. The next one might do more than stun. The lake sparkled in the twilight behind him and the hills rolled out like a carpet before him, but he couldn't see anything that could be used as shelter.

With nowhere to hide, he decided that he would have to make a run for it. He pulled himself back to his feet with a concentrated effort and stepped off in the direction of camp. He tried to run, but his equilibrium was still off. After three or four steps he came crashing back down to the ground, receiving a mouthful of sand for his efforts. It took Yens a few more seconds to compose himself before he was able to move again, but as soon as he could he pulled himself to his knees. His eyes were even slower to obey him, and he was on his knees for several seconds before they started to focus. When they did, he found himself staring directly as a thick pair of leather-strapped, hair-covered legs. Only inches away from him, they were holding up a powerful body that towered above his thin frame. A Wild One!

Yenspetsnicksnack fell backwards, scrambling on all fours to put as much distance as possible between him and the Wild One. The Wild One kicked Yens in the knees and then stepped on his midsection with one massive foot, effectively preventing any chance of escape. Yens felt desperately around the ground for something, anything, that could be used as a weapon but it was useless. His hands could only find sand and soft patches of grass.

The tall, mud-encrusted abomination of a man lifted a crude stone axe above his thick head and set to bring it down hard upon his captive.

Yens cringed, raising his hands to cover his eyes. He had read enough about the Wild Ones in the safety of his library back home to know that they never took prisoners. They were impossible to reason with, and without a weapon of any kind within reach, there was no chance to escape. His body tensed up and he held his breath as he awaited the inevitable. There could only be one outcome. Death.

A swishing sound sliced through the air, followed by the dull, sickening sound of ripping flesh. Yens opened his eyes with a start. The Wild One swayed back and forth and the axe dropped from lifeless fingers. The stone blade embedded deeply in the sand mere inches from Yens' face. The Wild One himself dropped moments later, landing on the mayor of Foran village and knocking the wind out of him. An arrow was wedged firmly in the center of its back.

"I did it!" a youthful voice said with a mixture of excitement and surprise. "I really did it. Are you all right, Yens?"

With an effort, the older man rolled the Wild One's bulky form to the side and sat up. Rodney, mounted on Credalis, was silhouetted in front of the last colorful strands of the sunset. Directly opposite the disappearing sun, two bright full moons were beginning to rise.

"I think so," Yens said as his breath returned to him. "Thank you, Rodney. You saved my life."

"Did you see that shot I made?"

"No, but now is not the time to sing of heroics. Wild Ones never travel alone. If there is one there will be others. Many others." Grunting and groaning, Yens struggled to his feet. "Did you bring my horse?"

"No," Rodney sheepishly admitted. "I was in such a hurry to rescue you that I didn't think to."

"No matter. I can ride with you."

"That's okay," a third voice said, joining the conversation. "I brought it, Rodney. That was a fun game too, but a little scary. At least it would have been, except that Ward's aren't scared of anything. So it must not have been scary at all, but it sure seemed like it was."

"Good for you, Ward," Rodney said, as he watched his friend dismount. Turning back to Yens, he added, "You see, I told you he'd be of use to us. Do you need any help getting on your horse?"

Yens waved Rodney away. He was still shaky and it took him three tries before he was able to throw himself in the saddle, but he was finally able to do it without assistance.

Rodney was about to tell Ward to climb up on Credalis with him when his attention was distracted by the sound of more approaching riders. He could clearly see Aimee and Gillian on the first horse to arrive, their young faces reflected in the moonlight. In the distance two more horses were heading in their direction, one riderless, and he rightly guessed it to be Ho-Don with the packhorses.

"It's good to see everyone alive," Ho-Don said without emotion as he brought the packhorses to a halt. The riderless horse stepped over to Ward and nuzzled him. Ward scratched the horse behind the ear before climbing onto her back. They were all mounted up again.

"What now?" Rodney asked, looking at Ho-Don. There was more than a touch of smugness in his voice, the inflection seeming to say *I was right and you were wrong.*

"We can't go back to the shelter of the trees now," Ho-Don said, ignoring Rodney's implied arrogance. "I've seen the firelight of at least eight Wild One camps scattered that way, and there are probably more."

"So?" Rodney questioned. "It's dark out. We should be able to ride around them without being seen."

"No," Yens said, shaking his head. "Wild Ones won't pursue us at night, but they do have sentries who patrol between their camps, and they will attack if we run into them. Believe me, even if we were at our best we would not have enough power to survive a battle with a sentry patrol."

"Then why don't we just stay here?"

"If we stay here we will be dead as soon as the sun rises. And since we can't go back, the only thing we can do is press on and pray we find some shelter in the mountains."

With only the light of the moons to guide them, they rode carefully along the side of the lake and made their way to the nearest mountain. Yens brought the group to a stop by the waterfall so they could examine their options. Water prevented them from moving along the base of the mountain in one direction. In the darkness, in the distance, they could see fires burning by the base in the other direction. They were against a wall with no direction to go but up.

"What about the horses?" Aimee asked when Yens made the decision to climb. "They'll never make it up that steep grade."

"Then they'll have to stay here," Yens answered. "I don't like it any more than you do, but we don't have a choice. Our only chance for survival is to put as much distance as we can between us and them because first thing in the morning the Wild Ones will be after us."

Aimee hugged herself to keep warm. Spray from the waterfall was slowly drenching them and a cool wind from the east was making her increasingly uncomfortable. With some reluctance she climbed off Ed.

At Yens' command, everyone took as much as they could easily carry and then made way to begin. The climb was very steep. Yens led the way, picking his footholds carefully. Rodney went second, followed by Ward, Aimee and Gillian, and finally Ho-Don. Progress was slow and, more often than not, they had to climb on all fours, using their hands to grab onto rocks and trees to pull themselves up. It was grueling work, and it wasn't long before the twins started to complain.

"I'm tired," Aimee said after about an hour of climbing. "We need to rest."

"We can't," Yens explained. "The farther we go before sun up, the less likely it is that the Wild Ones will be able to track us. We must keep moving."

"I don't care. I can't go any farther." Saying no more, Aimee sat down on a rock and refused to budge.

Yens rolled his eyes and muttered something under his breath, but once again he knew he had no chance of winning. He was in charge, but his plan would not work without the cooperation of the twins. If Aimee was going to be stubborn he had no choice. He would wait her out. But he wasn't going to just sit and do nothing as he waited. While the children rested, Yens ordered Ho-Don to go off searching in one direction and he went himself in the other. Climbing the mountain was still their only option, but perhaps they could find an easier path up.

Yens walked for about fifteen minutes, but he found the mountain to be just as steep and disagreeable the entire way. He turned back. Unless Ho-Don had found something, they would have to continue as they had been.

When Yens returned, the children were huddled together in an attempt to keep warm. Aimee was dozing off, but the others were wide awake despite the fact that they hadn't gotten any sleep in over twenty-four hours. Ho-Don was nowhere in sight. Blowing on his hands, Yens sat to wait with the others for the servant's return.

"I'm hungry," Rodney complained.

"I'm hungry too," added the Ward.

"We all are," Yens admitted. "When Ho-Don gets back I'll have him fix us something to tide us over before we continue. A few more minutes won't matter much. The Wild Ones won't chase us until morning."

"How come?"

"Because they're afraid to."

Rodney shook his head in amazement. "I can't believe those huge things would be afraid of anything."

"During the day they're not, but the nighttime is a different story. The Wild Ones are a very primitive people, you see, and their religion is as primitive as they are. They believe that the only reason we are put on this world is to fight and kill, and a warrior's worth is measured by how many other lives she or he has taken."

"That explains why they are after us," Aimee said. She had taken an interest in the story and forced herself to wake back up. "But I still don't understand why they won't come after us at night."

"I was getting to that. They also believe that a warrior's place in heaven is determined by how many people he kills before he himself is killed. The more lives you take, the greater your reward will be in the afterlife."

"That's sick."

"Indeed it is, Aimee, but they don't think so. They live their whole lives dedicated to this belief, killing to achieve the greatest reward possible in heaven. But the reward is only good if they make it to heaven."

Rodney thought this over for a few seconds. "That doesn't make any sense. One of the Ten Commandments is 'Thou shalt not kill', so if they do kill someone, they can never make it to heaven to collect their reward."

Yens smiled. "That is one of your God's commandments, but the Wild Ones worship another god, a war god. They call him Feroxx and say that he lives on the sun. According to their belief, when the Wild Ones die or are killed they are called home to live with Feroxx on the sun where they receive their reward for all the kills they have made throughout their lives. The more people they kill, the greater their reward, and it is the light of the sun that leads the warriors to their place in heaven. Now do you understand why they are afraid to fight at night?"

"Because there is no sun?"

"Very good, Rodney. Wild Ones are convinced that when the sun goes down it is Feroxx turning his back on the world. For this reason, they think that warriors that die at night are doomed. Without the light of the sun to lead them to Feroxx, the souls who die at night follow the only bright light available and end up on the moons. The moons are cold and barren and without reward, the domain of Feroxx's brother the lesser god Suroxx. The Wild Ones hide from the night in the safety of their camp and fight only during the day when Feroxx smiles upon them."

Yens took a breath and looked at his audience. The light of the moons reflected off their wide eyes as they stared back at him. Rodney, taking advantage of the silence, made a loud growling noise like that of a bear, while at the same time poking his sister in the side.

Aimee let out a shriek and jumped to her feet. Her heart still racing, she stared at her brother as her mind pieced together what had just happened. "That's not funny!" she scolded. Still shaky, she hugged herself tightly and stepped away from her Rodney.

"Was too funny," he said, laughing so hard that he rolled on his back. His laughter was contagious, at least as far as the Ward was concerned, and pretty soon the two of them were on their backs laughing and pointing at Aimee.

Gillian jumped to her feet and stood by her friend's side. "You men are every bit as evil as the teachings of Airia have led me to believe. How dare you taunt Aimee by playing upon her fears?"

The boys stopped laughing and sat back up. "It was just a joke," Rodney mumbled, his eyes focused on the ground. For some reason, Gillian's words hurt a lot more than they should have. "I didn't mean anything by it. Anyway, there's no such thing as Feroxx or Suroxx and no reason to be afraid of the dark. Anyone who is, is just plain dumb."

Gillian said no more. Rodney started to get to his feet but just as he was rising he heard a twig snap behind him and then a rustling in the bushes. Instinctively, he dove back for the ground, crouching low as he looked in the direction of the noise. This time it was Aimee's turn to laugh.

"What's so funny?" Ho-Don asked as he stepped from the bushes.

"Rodney's afraid of the dark."

"Am not," Rodney said as he jumped back up on his feet.

"Are too."

"Not."

"Too."

"Not."

"Enough" Yens ordered, silencing the twins. He turned to Ho-Don. "Did you find a path?"

The servant shook his head.

"Very well, then. We will eat and then continue on the way we have been going."

Ho-Don set to work while the children huddled back together to keep warm. Suddenly and without warning, Ward jumped up and ran off into the night. Rodney called after him, but it was of no use. He was gone.

"I told you he'd be trouble," Yens said as Ho-Don dished out strips of jerky that were about the only food that wasn't lost in the Dismal Forest. "Let's eat and get moving. I still want to make as much progress as possible by morning."

"But Ward…"

"He's gone, Rodney, and there's nothing any of us can do to find him. Knowing how stupid Wards are, he's probably forgotten all about us by now. The most we can do is move ahead and hope that he is able to avoid the Wild Ones on his own. Now let's get going."

CHAPTER THIRTEEN
The Crown of Fortis

They felt a little refreshed, but not much. The short rest only left them wanting more, but Yens wouldn't allow that. He insisted they keep moving.

The climb itself continued to be difficult and they proceeded in silence. Yens was busy blazing the trail, the girls were both too tired to talk, and Ward's disappearance had Rodney sulking. He couldn't believe that his friend had just taken off like that without saying a word. There had to be some explanation, some reason for his doing what he did. But no. Ward was gone and there was nothing Rodney could do about it. He couldn't even understand why.

An hour passed. Then two, and three. Lack of sleep was taking its toll on everyone. Aimee stumbled three times, the last time scraping her leg against a rock and drawing blood. Gillian watched with surprise as Rodney gently cleaned the area and bandaged it up with a strip of cloth that he ripped from his own shirt. When he was finished he looked up at Yens. "We need sleep. We have to stop and rest."

"I know," Yens agreed, "but we have to keep moving. If we stop here we will freeze, and if we build a fire to keep warm the Wild Ones will see it from below and will know where to find us in the morning. I don't like it any more that you do, but we don't have another choice."

"How about if we hide the fire behind some rocks or something? Maybe they won't be able to see it, then."

Yens shook his head. "Even if the fire can't be seen directly, it's reflection off the trees overhead will give our position away."

"We could build a fire in the cave where the Wild Ones won't be able to see it. We should go there, it isn't far. And then we can be both hidden and warm."

Every head turned toward the new yet familiar voice.

"Ward!" Rodney exclaimed, running to his friend and hugging him. "Where have you been?"

"In the cave," he said as they broke the embrace. From his tone it was obvious that he expected everyone to already know that.

"What cave?"

"The cave that Ward and I used to play in several years ago. We used to play all kinds of games inside it. What kind of games do you like to play, Rodney?"

Yens grabbed Ward by the shoulders and looked him in the eye. "Forget about the games. If there is a cave nearby you must take us there immediately."

"Okay," Ward smiled. Shaking himself free of Yens he headed back the way he had just come, walking slow and easy. The cave was as close by as he had said it was, and they were there within a matter of minutes. Rigging up a torch, Yens led the way inside. The mouth of the cave was small and they had to go in one at a time, but it opened up quickly and they were able to stand together as a group inside. Icicle-shaped stalactites hung down from the ceiling while stalagmites stood tall on the cavern floor, but there was still plenty of room. The rocky walls were wet with condensation on either side, but the cavern was so deep that the torch could not penetrate all the way back. A large pile of wood was neatly stacked along one of the side walls.

"I put the wood there," Ward eagerly volunteered, "so we can build a fire. I like being warm. Don't you, Rodney?"

Yens took a handful of kindling and set it on the stone floor. He touched his torch to it and soon a hot blaze was stealing the chill from the front of the cave. Yens was surprised to note that the stupid Ward was smart enough to only bring in wood from the Cassel tree, a tree native to the Barrier Mountains that was virtually smokeless when burned, so there was no trouble with lack of ventilation.

The fire was a welcome addition, and the weary children huddled around it while Yens and Ho-Don went outside to prepare for the eventuality that the Wild Ones might track them to the cave.

"I'm hungry again," Aimee said as she warmed her hands by the fire. They had been sitting there in silence for several minutes, and she was stretching for a topic of conversation. "Maybe when Ho-Don is finished out there he can give us some more of that beef jerky."

"Tell him not to get any for me," Rodney returned. "I'm not hungry."

Aimee was surprised by this. She had never known her brother to refuse food before, and she told him so.

"I was just thinking about Feroxx, the god of the Wild Ones," Rodney said in way of an answer. "I know they believe in killing to get to their version of heaven, but we've always been told that killing is a sin. Well, we've been so busy running for our lives that I haven't had time to think about it until now, but I killed someone today. When I shot that arrow into the Wild One's back I broke one of the Ten Commandments." He picked up a stone and casually tossed it into the fire. "Does this mean that I'm going to go to Hell?"

Aimee stumbled for an answer, but the best she could do was shrug her shoulders.

"You did what you had to do," Gillian interjected. "If you hadn't acted quickly like that, Yens, and perhaps all of us, would now be dead. By taking one evil life, you saved several good ones. Surely no just God could condemn you for that."

"If we succeed in our mission," Yens added as he returned to the cave, "that one act will end up saving thousands of lives, perhaps even more. Believe me, boy, you did the right thing." Yens wiped a bead of sweat from his forehead and sat down by the fire. Ho-Don, standing beside him, did the same.

"You look exhausted," Aimee said, looking at Yens from across the fire. "What did you just do?"

"Built a trap that, hopefully, won't be needed," Yens answered. He took inventory of the tired and scared faces of the children before him. Rodney and Aimee were sitting close to each other, almost too afraid to move. Gillian sat on Aimee's other side, clutching her bow tightly as if trying to draw strength from it. Her entire way of life had been stolen from her, and now she faced possible death at the hands of sub-human, unthinking creatures. Only Ward showed no fear. Grinning like an imbecile, he stared at the fire as if hypnotized by it, completely ignoring what was being said.

"How about a story," Yens continued, trying to take their minds off the immediate threat.

"Could you tell us more about Airia?" Aimee pleaded.

"No," argued Rodney. "You already told us a long story about Airia. I want to hear more about Fortis."

At the mention of Fortis, Ward looked up from the fire and for the first time began to take an interest in the conversation. "Who's Fortis?" he wanted to know.

Yens glanced at the grinning simpleton with disgust, but that didn't stop him from answering the question. "Fortis was the first king of the Truculans. Though just a boy, he did what many men had failed to do. He united the warring tribes and established the nation that ruled Daak wisely and justly for more than a dozen centuries until they were destroyed by Haeron.

"No one really knows where Fortis came from. It is said that he just appeared one day in the midst of the Quabi'il at a time when the Truculans were on the verge of destroying themselves."

"What's a Quabi'il?"

"One of the many tribes that eventually merged to become the Truculan nation, the one that Fortis was adopted into. When he first appeared the tribes were all at war, and even within some of the tribes brothers were fighting brothers and sons battling against fathers to gain power and stature in the weird hierarchy that existed before the coming of Fortis.

"It is said that Fortis put an end to all this warring by uniting the tribes against a common enemy, the mad god Azamath, with the help of Archimagus."

"The same Archimagus that we're looking for now?" Rodney was astonished to think that he could still be alive after thousands of years.

"Yes, his magic has sustained him all this time, though he was little more than a fledgling then. It was Archimagus that gave Fortis the mystical crown that he wore into battle when he led the tribes against Azamath's forces. The ancient Truculan legends held that the crown had the power to stop any foe, but only the chosen one could harness its power. Fortis was that chosen one.

"Bravely he faced Azamath, and the crown did just as legend said it would. Fortis unleashed its power and the mad god was defeated but not without loss. When the dust cleared, there was no sign of Fortis or the crown. Some say that Fortis sacrificed himself to save the tribes while others contend that he merely returned to that strange and mystical place he had come from. Either way, most people on Daak believe that he will someday return and reunite with Archimagus, and the two of them will save Daak in its hour of greatest need. It is also believed that anyone who finds the crown of Fortis will gain its power and become ruler of all the planet."

If I had that crown now, I'd walk right into Haeron's castle and kick her butt," announced Rodney, speaking through a yawn.

Yens smiled. "Go to sleep. No matter what happens, we're going to have a long day tomorrow, so it's time to rest." Getting up, he walked to the mouth of the cave to watch the fires of the Wild Ones on the fields below. Soon, deep breathing and gentle snoring told him that he was the only one still awake.

* * *

Yens spent the night in exactly that position and eventually fell asleep right in the mouth. Shortly before dawn he awoke. Rising, he quietly checked the children to make sure that they were sleeping before waking Ho-Don. Using hand signals, he instructed his servant to take over the watch by the mouth and then reached into his bag. He dug out the crystal that Haeron had given him and walked into the depths of the cave. When he was satisfied that he was well out of sight and sound of the children he gently set the crystal on a rocky ledge and flipped it's switch on.

"Where have you been, you stinking piece of dung?" screamed a woman's voice.

"I apologize, my queen," Yens humbly replied, averting his eyes to avoid her stare. He quickly explained the trouble that they had encountered, first with the Sisterhood of Airia and then with the Wild Ones. "With a little luck," he concluded, "the Wild Ones won't pursue us and we'll be able to continue our journey to Frieer in a couple of hours."

"And if they find you in that cave?"

"Ho-Don and I have prepared some defenses. With a little luck we should be able to hold them off until nightfall and then escape into the darkness."

"You had better be correct, worm. You are already behind schedule. Any further delay is unacceptable. The head of Archimagus must hang on the end of my scepter before the beginning of the Mid-Summer's feast! If you disappoint me, I will see to it that there is room for your head on my scepter as well."

Yens shuddered. "Your orders will be carried out with the swiftness of a gazelle," he responded as meekly as possible. "My only desire is to see that your will is done."

"As well it should be, toad." Without another word, Haeron flipped her communication crystal off. Her image had barely faded when Yens was distracted by a dull thud followed by a whimper of pain. He hurried to the source of the sound and found Ho-Don standing over the crumpled form of the Ward. A trickle of blood was running down the side of the Ward's head.

"How much did he hear?"

"Enough. What do you wish me to do with him?"

"The moron probably isn't smart enough to understand anything he heard much less remember it, but why take chances? Throw him outside the cave and make sure you toss the body somewhere out of sight. By the time he wakes up, if he wakes up, we should be long gone. And the children will never know what happened."

Ho-Don nodded. "May I speak plainly, Master?"

"If you must."

"I do not wish to criticize your activities, my Lord…"

"Then don't."

"It's just that you seem to be growing rather attached to the children. I would think that this might complicate matters when it comes time to turn them over to Haeron."

Yens bit his lower lip. "I'll keep that in mind. Now do as you're told and take care of that idiot. And be quick about it. It's almost time to wake the children and I want you to have a hot meal ready and waiting for them."

Ho-Don looked at him curiously.

"Don't be a fool," Yens snapped. "If the Wild Ones attack it will be a difficult battle, and we will all need to be operating at our peak. Now carry out your orders. This discussion is over."

CHAPTER FOURTEEN
Into the Mountain

"This is delicious, Ho-Don," Rodney said as he shoveled another spoonful into his mouth. "What do you call it?"

"It's name is aldine, but what it really is, is tree stew. The woods outside the cave are full of the sweet-barked trees. Would you like seconds?"

Rodney held his bowl out and nodded his head eagerly. "Has anybody seen Ward? I know he would like this stuff."

"The fool probably wandered off again. Forget about him, he was nothing but trouble anyway."

"No way," Rodney answered indignantly. "I'm going to look for him."

"That's not such a good idea," Gillian answered, joining the conversation. She was eating her aldine by the mouth of the cave. "Come take a look."

Like a small school of fish, Yens, Ho-Don and the twins moved as one to the entrance and looked out. The sun had risen, and the bottom half of the mountain was now swarming with Wild Ones bearing crude spears and axes. They were heading directly for the cave.

Yens twisted his neck and barked his orders to the children. "It looks like this is it. I want all of you to move as far back as you can and wait."

Without another word, Yens and Ho-Don slipped out into the open. Before the children even had a chance to wonder what they were doing, the two men dove back into the cave, hugging the rock floor as if their lives depended on it. Outside, a sound like a collapsing building rained down the side of the mountain, kicking up tons of dirt and filth.

"What was that?" Aimee asked, choking on the dust that was now hanging thick in the air.

"That was the trap that Ho-Don and I built last night," Yens answered. "We collected all the rocks and fallen logs and everything else we could find and piled them so that they would create a rockslide when set into motion."

The group gathered around the mouth to see if the slide was effective, but the dust obscured their view. They had to wait several minutes before they were able to make anything out.

Suddenly, a hairy form came into immediate focus, popping up in the cave entrance and slithering through the opening before anyone could react.

Once inside, the Wild One reared up to its full height and waved an axe at the group. With an inhuman bellow, it raised the stone axe above its head and swung it hard at Yens. Reacting more by instinct than design, Yens rolled onto the cave floor to avoid the swipe of the axe. At the same time, he thrust his staff into the air, ramming its end into the creature's left eye. The Wild One staggered for a second, dropping the axe as it lifted both hands to cradle its wound.

Ho-Don swooped towards the fallen axe, but the creature saw him coming with its one good eye and reached out for the smaller man. Grabbing Ho-Don by the neck, the Wild One began to squeeze with all its strength. Ho-Don tried to wiggle free, but it was no use. His face looked like one huge blood blister about to pop, and he tried pounding at the creature's hands, but it was no use. His body went limp in the monster's grasp.

Back on his feet, Yens ran at the creature. Holding his staff in both hands he swung at the Wild One, but this time the beast was ready. Tossing Ho-Don's unmoving body aside, the Wild One grabbed the end of Yens' staff and used the weapon against its owner, pushing him hard against a thick stalagmite. Yens hit the slick protrusion with a crack and dropped to the floor only a couple of feet from the still unmoving body of his servant.

The Wild One reared its head back and let out a victory roar, its loud shout echoing throughout the chambers of the cave. Then it noticed the children.

Aimee, Rodney and Gillian were all backed against one wall of the cave, half hidden in shadows. Their bows were all setting across the cavern on the far wall. The creature roared again, louder this time, glaring at the children with its one good eye as it bellowed in their direction. The children shuddered, partly from fear but mostly from disgust at the foul stench that came blasting from the brute's mouth. It was still clutching Yens' staff in its hairy paws.

Aimee glanced across the cave to where their bows and arrows were setting. At least twenty feet away, there was no way to get to them without being caught by the Wild One first. "Maybe if we all run," she suggested, "at least one of us will make it."

"Maybe," Rodney agreed, "but maybe there's a better way. Why don't I distract him, and while he's busy you try to sneak over there. I don't think he can hit my fast ball."

"What are you talking about?"

"Just go," Rodney said as he bent over and scooped up four small rocks. Stepping out of the shadows, he stood to face the creature. "And Shuster's one out away from a perfect game," Rodney said out loud. The beast tilted its head, not sure what was going on. Blood continued to drip from the one eye. The other was now completely focused on Rodney.

"Here's the wind-up, and the pitch," Rodney continued, hiding one of the rocks in his hand as he kicked his left leg high in the air. Coming back down on his leg, he threw the rock as hard as he could at the creature. The Wild One itself, more out of reflex than anything else, took an off-balance swipe at the rock with Yens' staff. He missed.

"Strike one!" Rodney shouted as he palmed another rock. This time, as Rodney began his wind-up, Aimee started for the weapons. Rodney launched the rock and again the beast swung the staff. Again it missed.

"Strike two!" Rodney cheered as the rock sailed out the mouth of the cave. "One more strike and we win the pennant!"

Aimee ducked behind a stalagmite, half-way to the bows and waited for Rodney to throw the next rock. He did, and again the Wild One swiped at it, but this time the off-balance swing forced the savage to stumble. When the Wild One recovered, it was now standing directly between her and the weapons. Aimee glanced helplessly at her brother and Rodney, for his part, looked back at her for a suggestion. But it was Gillian who spoke next.

"Give me that," she said, taking the last stone out of the boy's hands. Like Rodney before her, she too threw the stone at the beast, but she was focusing on a different target. Her aim was true, and with a thud the rock hit the savage in the right eye. Now completely blind, the creature's scream was deafening and it backed away in pain. Gillian watched as the Wild One, dropping the staff to clutch both hands over its eyes, continued to back off. Just as it passed by the entrance of the cave, the sister of Airia took a running start and heaved her body into the air, landing a two-footed kick on the beast's chest.

Gillian dropped to the stone floor, rolling as she landed. But more importantly, the momentum of the kick pushed the creature out of the cave, and its massive form went tumbling down the mountain.

Rodney poked his head out the mouth of the cave and watched as the creature bounced down the mountain, bellowing the whole way. "I don't know what he's so sore about," he said to Gillian. "You hit him with the pitch. He gets to take his base."

Gillian nodded, pretending to understand what he meant by that.

The debris of the landslide set in motion a couple of minutes ago was now piled at the base of the mountain. Scattered among the rocks and fallen trees were the broken bodies of dozens of Wild Ones. The survivors of the carnage gathered together, circling the area excitedly and occasionally pointing toward the cave, but none made a move in its direction.

"That's it," Rodney said, slapping his hands together. "We've shown them who's boss. Now let's find Ward and get on with our mission."

"Not so fast," Yens warned. Recovering his staff, he used it to slowly pull himself back to his feet. Nearby, Ho-Don was also trying to stand back up. "The Wild Ones are going to do one of two things. They will either resume the attack or decide that it is impossible to reach us and go away. Hopefully they'll leave, but if they attack and we've left the safety of this cave, we won't stand a chance. We have to wait them out."

* * *

"This is crazy," Rodney complained. The sun was now high in the sky. "They haven't moved for hours. I wish something would happen."

"This seems to be your lucky day," Yens said in a voice thick with sarcasm as he looked down the mountain. "Your wish has been granted. Here they come."

"What do we do now?"

"Now it gets tricky. You children take up position at the mouth and keep them away for as long as you can."

Doing as they were told, the three children stood side by side and nocked arrows in their bowstrings. Taking aim, they waited until the nearest of the rushing hordes came into range and then let their arrows fly. The Wild Ones continued their charge despite the deadly projectiles whistling through the air, but their progress was slowed considerably. Gillian's aim was flawless, and while the twins didn't manage to score a direct hit with every shot their percentage was incredible considering that they had less than two weeks training.

Unfortunately, there were a great many more of the enemy than there were arrows and it wasn't long before they had exhausted their supply. The children had thinned down the number of attackers, but they weren't able to turn them back.

"Get behind us!" Yens screamed to the children. "Ho-Don and I will handle things from here. I want the three of you to go as far into the cave as you possibly can and hide in the darkness. The Wild Ones are as stupid as they are savage. If Ho-Don and I fail they might assume that we were alone and leave without searching the cave."

"We can't just leave you like this," Rodney cried.

Yens spun on his heels and shot Rodney such a dark look that it made him shiver. "You can and you will. Now do as you are told. Go."

The two men took up position while the children disappeared into the depths of the cavern. They didn't have long to wait for the battle to begin. Fortunately, the mouth of the cave was narrow which made it impossible for more than one Wild one to get inside at a time, and even then they had to crouch to do so. This gave Yens and Ho-Don the advantage of being able to strike whenever one of the savages appeared, while they were still off-balance and not in positions to defend themselves. Yens with his quarter staff and Ho-Don with a dagger in each hand proved to be an effective team and for nearly an hour they were able to beat back every invader that entered the mouth of the cave.

In the end, though, they faced the same problem of numbers that the children did. They were only two. The enemy was many. Eventually, they began to tire and the Wild Ones started pushing them back. It looked as if death was imminent, and to make matters worse Rodney came running back into the chaos.

"I told you, uhhn, to stay hidden," Yens snapped at the boy between thrusts of his staff. "This battle has become hopeless. You had a chance to wait it out in the safety of the shadows, but now you must stay and die with us to protect your sister."

Rodney shrugged his shoulders. "You can stay and die if you want, but I'm escaping with the girls through a secret door we found in the back of the cave. I just thought that you might want to come with us."

"You found a way out?"

"Duh. Now are you coming or what?"

Disengaging, the men chased after Rodney, following him back toward the rear of the cavern. The Wild Ones were as slow as they were bulky. Rodney, Yens and Ho-Don gained a marginal lead as they slipped into the cover of darkness. Just as it was becoming impossible to see, they noticed a beacon of green light in the distance. It was a doorway, just as Rodney had said.

"Here we come," the boy shouted. As soon as they stepped through the threshold, Aimee and Gillian slammed the door shut and slid a locking mechanism into place. The Wild Ones pounded on the other side of the door, but it stood strong.

For the moment they were safe.

* * *

The cavernous tunnel stretched out in front of them for what seemed like miles. Though dark and uninviting, they had no choice but to follow its lead. To go back meant certain death. The stone floor sloped gently downward, leading them into the heart of the mountain. The walls glowed with the same strange green light that had allowed Rodney to find the door in the first place. The light was dim, casting shadows into the depths of the tunnel. Dim, but bright enough for them to see where they were going.

The floor of the tunnel was clear of obstruction and wide enough to allow them to walk two abreast. Occasionally they came to a bend in the cavern that turned them completely around, but it continued to lead them downward to whatever lie waiting for them below. Somewhere around what Yens guessed to be midday he called a halt for lunch at a bend in the path.

They sat for a long time in the dim glow, listening to the distant dripping and rushing of an unseen spring while Ho-Don prepared their meal. Actually, there was nothing for him to prepare. They had left in such a hurry that all he had time to grab was a chunk of aldine bark and the backpack with the jerky in it. He handed out the strips of meat first, and while they were being eaten he broke the aldine apart and distributed it. It was not as good raw as it was cooked, but it did have a bitter-sweet taste that was palatable.

"I don't understand," Rodney said, looking around. "The green light seems to be everywhere, but I can't tell what's causing it. It's spooky."

Yens took a bite of aldine and coughed. There was no water to wash the food down with, and he had difficulty swallowing the last bite. "I know what causes it, and I don't like it one bit," he said between coughs. "There's only one thing that makes such a pale green light – magic. Very powerful magic."

"Magic," Aimee repeated, saying it like it was a brand new word that she was trying out for the first time. "Is it from the evil Sorceress?"

"I don't know and I don't want to wait around long enough to find out. Finish up and we'll be on our way."

Moments later they were walking down the passageway again. Rodney glanced back at where they had eaten lunch and startled. "Um, Yens, I don't want to worry you or anything, but the green light isn't shining behind us anymore."

"I know," he answered without looking back himself. "It would seem that the power behind the light is leading us somewhere. I've also noticed that we've passed several side tunnels that we could have turned on to, but only the one we're on continues to be lit. Whoever is behind all this seems to be guiding us in a very specific direction."

They walked for the better part of the day, but between the winding of the passage and the unchanging design of the floor and walls it didn't seem that they were getting anywhere. About three hours after lunch, though, the tunnel slowly opened up and the green light began to grow brighter. Presently they found themselves standing in a huge cavern. Despite the fact that they had traveled miles beneath the surface, the light was so intense here that it was as bright as day.

The group paused to look the cavern over. Stalagmites and stalactites joined together throughout the underground room, forming a strange pattern that seemed almost planned. In the center of it all was an ornate throne carved out of solid rock. Something was etched into the side of the throne, but Rodney and Aimee were unable to read the scratchings. If the marks were indeed writing, it wasn't in English or any other language or alphabet the twins had ever heard of. It looked like a bunch of scribbles.

On the seat of the throne rested a thick gold band, large enough to place on a head, inlaid with five sparkling gemstones.

"Is that what I think it is?" Rodney asked.

Yens bent down to study the strange script on the side of the throne. "It's in the language of the elders," he explained in an awed whisper. "I can't make it all out, but I can understand enough. This is the Crown of Fortis."

"Then what are we waiting for?" Aimee wanted to know. "With this we'll be able to defeat Haeron ourselves and save the planet right away. We won't even need to find Archimagus."

"No," Yens answered, shoving Aimee roughly to the ground. "With this crown *I* can defeat Haeron and rule Daak for myself."

Rodney moved toward his fallen sister, but before he could get far he too was knocked to the ground. It wasn't Yens who had pushed him down, however. It was the ground itself. Rodney forced himself back to his feet, but his effort was futile. The ground was still shaking and he was thrown right back down. The rumbling of the quake grew louder, and Rodney heard the sound of tearing stone beneath where he had fallen. The ground was splitting right below him. He tried to scramble away to safety, but it was no use. The hole was opening up too fast and he was sliding right in. Rodney managed to grab a handhold on the edge of the newly formed crevice, but his grip was precarious at best. His body dangled over what seemed to be a bottomless pit and he didn't know how long he could hold on.

The quake continued, and the crevice that threatened to engulf Rodney grew in either direction. On one side it stopped harmlessly in front of a stalagmite, but in the other direction it butted up against and then split the rock throne that held the Crown of Fortis. The Crown was tossed off the throne and bounced twice on the stone floor. As the rumbling of the quake ended, the Crown rolled to the crevice and then came to a stop, balancing on the edge of the pit, ready to fall in at any second.

Yens moved toward the Crown but was stopped by Rodney's desperate voice. "Help me. I can't hold on any longer."

Turning from the Crown, Yens saw Rodney about to fall into the same crevice that was threatening to engulf the diadem. He had time to save only one. Conflicting images flew before his mind's eye at lightning speed. He saw himself wearing the Crown of Fortis, ruling the entire planet, his iron hand crushing all who opposed him. Then he saw himself helpless on the ground, about to be killed by the Wild One. The image of Rodney on top of Credalis with the sunset behind him was burned forever on Yens' mind. Rodney had risked his life to save Yens then…

Yens made his decision. Diving toward the boy, he reached down and grasped Rodney's hand, pulling him safely back to solid ground even as the Crown tumbled into the abyss. The two of them rested, breathless, on the lip of the crevice. Yens started to relax, but a scream from Aimee put him on the alert again.

"Traitor,' Ho-Don spat. He was standing above Yens with a knife gripped firmly in his hand. "You could have had the Crown of Fortis. With it, Mistress Haeron would have been able to solidify her rule over Daak and no one, not even Archimagus, would be able to harm her. But you let it slip away to save this worthless boy. I warned you, but you wouldn't listen. Now you shall die for your indiscretion."

"Wait, Ho-Don," pleaded Yens.

"No. I've already waited too long. The dark Sorceress had her doubts about your loyalty from the start. She installed me secretly as your servant so I could ensure that you carried out her wishes. I should have killed you in your sleep days ago when I first realized how attached you were becoming to these children but I foolishly thought you might come to your senses. Now it is too late. Prepare to die."

Ho-Don made his move in a flash. Lunging in the other man's direction, he thrust his knife at Yens' chest. Yens rolled to the side and the dagger struck the stone floor with a dull clang. The children, confused by what was happening, clustered together across the chamber and watched.

In another moment both men were back on their feet facing each other. Ho-Don waved his dagger menacingly in the air. Yens kept one eye on his adversary and looked desperately around for his staff with the other. It was too far away. His only hope was to wrest the knife away. Circling Ho-Don, he waited for an opening. When the moment came he leapt, wrapping the fingers of his right hand around the wrist holding the dagger. Ho-Don used his free hand to punch Yens in the face, hoping to knock him away, but Yens held on.

The punch did, however, stagger Yens and he realized that if Ho-Don got in another one, he would be finished. Grabbing Ho-Don's shirt with his other arm he closed the distance between their two bodies. Holding tight, the knife became useless and the fight became a wrestling match.

Ho-Don tried to swing around and shake Yens off, but all he managed to accomplish was to knock the two of them, still grasping for the knife, to the ground. They rolled back and forth. First Yens was on top. Then Ho-Don. But neither was able to get the dagger away from the other. Their rolling took them to the edge of the crevice and they came to a stop with Ho-Don again on top. Yens was on his back, his head and shoulders hanging over the edge.

Ho-Don yanked hard, wrenching his knife hand away from Yens. He held the dagger high in the air and fixed a stony gaze at Yens. "It ends here."

The knife came slicing down, but Yens was not defeated yet. In a last-ditch effort he reached up and caught Ho-Don's wrist in mid swing. With a twist of his own, the knife changed course and plunged deep into Ho-Don's chest. After staring briefly into the now unseeing eyes of his former servant, Yens shoved the unmoving body off of him and stood up.

"Very good, Lord Mayor," a voice cried out from above the chamber. It was followed by clapping that echoed dully throughout the chamber. The Ward, his head bandaged, was standing on the ledge of a small cliff. There was no sign of his ever-present smile and his eyes sparkled with sharp intelligence. He climbed down from the ledge and approached the group slowly.

"What's going on here?" Demanded Yens.

"Your confusion is understandable," Ward answered. "Be grateful that you are still alive to be confused. If you had chosen to go for the Crown instead of Rodney, you would now be as dead as your servant."

"Yens isn't the only one here who's confused," Rodney said as the children approached. "I don't understand anything that just went on here."

Instead of responding to the statement, Ward turned toward Rodney and dropped to one knee. "Welcome back to Daak, my Lord Fortis."

CHAPTER FIFTEEN
Archimagus

"What in the world are you talking about?" Rodney asked, stepping back from the Ward.

"And for that matter, Ward," interjected Aimee, "how come you're talking so smart all of a sudden?"

"Things are not always as they seem," Ward told them as he stood, "nor have they ever been. You thought you knew me as a stupid Ward, but that was a disguise all along. I am and always have been Archimagus and you, friend Rodney, are my liege, King Fortis of Daak, Lord of the Truculans. I met you in days long past and we were friends and allies. You taught me my first magic - a simple spell, but one that forged my destiny. You befriended my father and united the tribes. You saved Daak from destruction then, and have now returned to help us again in this, our hour of greatest need. Prophesy is being fulfilled even as we speak."

"Look," Rodney began, "I don't know what this is all about, but I do know that I'm not Fortis. I never saw you before we met a couple of days ago when you were a stupid Ward. Now all of a sudden you are trying to tell me that I'm a king and you're the person we've been searching for all along? If all this is true, why didn't you tell me about it when we first met?"

"I'm sorry for tricking you, but I really didn't have any other choice. I recognized you instantly, Rodney, but since you didn't know who I truly was and I had no idea who the others were I decided to wait until I discovered the truth about everyone before I could reveal my true identity."

"And what truths did you discover, magician?" Yens wanted to know.

Archimagus looked blankly at Yens. "Do you really need to ask that question?"

"He may not need to, but I sure do," Aimee stated. "What did you find out?"
"Ho-Don may have been Yens' servant, but he was also a servant of the dark sorceress Haeron," Archimagus answered, turning toward Rodney and the girls. "And so is our friend the mayor here."

"That's a lie," Rodney screamed. "Yens may be a bit of a pain now and then, but he's one of the good guys. He's our friend and he'd never work for someone so evil. Tell him, Yens. Tell him that he's got it all wrong."

Yenspetsnicksnack opened his mouth and then closed it again. Shifting from one foot to the other, he shuffled uneasily as he searched for the right words. A dozen lies popped into his head, but he pushed them all aside.

"I'm afraid he's telling the truth," Yens finally said. "The only reason that I brought you children to this world was to trap Archimagus and help Haeron's armies find and destroy the Hidden People. With the descendants of the Truculans defeated and you children safely in her grasp there would be no one .to challenge her power. In return she promised to make me governor of all Atalan."

"There is no trusting men, sister," interrupted Gillian. "They are the enemy. They know neither honor nor truth and exist only to deceive."

The twins were crushed and Yens was filled with shame, but he ignored Gillian's comments and continued. "I have always craved power and the only way that it seemed possible to achieve any power worth having in this dark age on Daak was to ally myself with Haeron. Unfortunately, I didn't know just how evil she truly was until it was too late. By then my fate was sealed to hers and she would have killed me without pause if she even suspected that I was disloyal."

"Do you seek to compound your treachery with more lies?" Archimagus asked with a glare in his eye. "Was it too late when you enslaved your fellow villagers? Was it too late when you ordered Ho-Don to take me out of the cave and get rid of me? You are evil, Lord Mayor, and the only reason that you did not share Ho-Don's fate is that you chose to save Rodney over seizing the Crown. If you had gone for it instead, your body now be heaped alongside your servant's."

"You're right," Yens admitted. "I have acted evilly. My cowardice forced me to forsake the trust that my people had placed upon me, but I'm not the man I was. A few weeks ago these two innocents entered my life and altered it forever. Rodney, Aimee, you were so trusting, so loving that I found myself changing, beginning to care for you. It wasn't a sudden change, I admit. When you first came to Daak I would have been just as happy to hand you over to Haeron right then, but I had promised to use you as bait to capture Archimagus. Then, during your training and the journey, I realized that I was learning to respect and envy the qualities you possess and this made it difficult to contemplate fulfilling my duties to Haeron.

"But I would have fulfilled them. More out of fear for my own safety than out of loyalty, but I would have fulfilled them none-the-less. I would have delivered you to her in bondage if I hadn't been found out. I am a power-hungry coward."

"So you say," Aimee reasoned, "but I don't believe it. You fought bravely this morning when the Wild Ones attacked us in the cave, risking your own life to protect ours, and right now you're admitting the truth to us where a true coward would still be lying to protect himself. And as for being power-hungry, you let the Crown of Fortis, which could have made you ruler of all Daak, fall into the crevice while you saved my brother's life."

Yens shrugged his shoulders. "It was the only thing I could do. Rodney saved my life by the lake yesterday when the Wild One was about to kill me. I couldn't let him die when it was within my power to save him."

Yens breathed deeply, not knowing what else to say. Aimee took the initiative. She wrapped her arms around him and squeezed him tightly. "When you first brought us to Daak I didn't think that you were telling us the whole truth. I knew that you weren't all good then, and I know that you're not all bad now."

Yens returned Aimee's hug. "Perhaps you are right. Maybe it's not too late for me after all. I'm ready to redeem myself. With your permission, I would like to stay with you and help you fight Haeron."

"No," Rodney shouted. His face was flushed and his cheeks were stained with tears. "No," he said again, this time a little more softly.

"You lied to us. You lied to me. I trusted you, Yens. When we first came here and Aimee tried to tell me that something was wrong I argued with her. I convinced her that you were our friend. Now I find out that the whole time I was defending you, you were plotting to use us and then turn us over to Haeron. I'm sorry, but no. I don't think that I can ever trust you again."

Gillian placed a hand on the boy's shoulder and just as quickly removed it. "Rodney is right. This scum of a man betrayed us once. There is no reason to believe that he won't do so again. The Crown of Fortis is gone and the only way he can achieve the power he covets now is through the dark Sorceress. We should kill him now while we have the chance."

Aimee looked at the newly-revealed magician. "It's just a feeling, and I don't have anything to back it up with, but I think Yens can be trusted."

Archimagus nodded slightly. "One of the traits that I have found over the years to be important is that of forgiveness, and Yenspetsnicksnack's words have the ring of truth to them. He is also the only one among us that has been inside Haeron's castle. It would be to our mutual benefit if we let him continue on the mission."

"And if you're wrong?"

"Then we're all doomed, but I don't see any alternative. Without him, we will never get inside her fortress."

A slight breeze whispered through the tunnel echoing the silence that their conversation had lapsed into. Aimee looked to Rodney for a reaction to Archimagus' decision. He scuffled his feet along the rock floor of the tunnel and swayed back and forth nervously for several seconds before speaking finally through clenched teeth. "If that's the way it has to be, that's the way it has to be. But I don't like it."

"Nor do I," Gillian firmly added.

"So, Archimagus," Aimee said loudly, trying to change the focus of the discussion. "How come you look like a Ward and acted as stupidly as a Ward up until now? You just using this as a disguise or something?"

"Very perceptive," Archimagus said with a straight face. He spoke some strange, unintelligible words, and a blinding light appeared out of nowhere and engulfed him. As quickly as it came it disappeared, and where the eternally young Ward had been standing there was now a tall, handsome adult. His light blonde hair framed a youthful-looking, almost cherubic, face with twinkling brown eyes, and a well-defined nose. The smile that now graced that face was as full and as friendly as the Ward's ever was. If the others didn't know that the man before them was thousands of years old, they wouldn't have guessed him to be a day over twenty.

"A long time ago, when Haeron was first consolidating her power in Daak," the man went on to say, "I was warned that one of her first steps would be to annihilate the Truculans as we were the law keepers, the power of justice in those days. I was much younger then and very foolish. I had met her once before and was not impressed by her abilities so I dismissed these warnings and failed to keep an eye on her. Because of this I was unprepared when she suddenly attacked.

"In less than a day her forces overran and captured nearly a quarter of the planet, killing every magic user that they encountered. Sedes, the capital city of the Truculan Empire, was the first to fall and was completely destroyed. It was just by dumb luck that I escaped that fate.

"I was away studying in the mountains when Sedes was annihilated and as a result I was the only Truculan leader who wasn't killed by Haeron that day. When word about what happened reached me it was too late to do anything but gather the other Truculan survivors together and assess our losses. Some of us wanted to fight back, but I realized that there were so few of us we wouldn't have stood a chance. The only thing we could do was to go into hiding and bide our time, and since the best place to hide is in a crowd I used my magic to disguise the entire Truculan race as Wards and we dispersed throughout Daak. We then began spreading rumors of an imaginary hidden city someplace in the frozen land of Frieer where the Truculans were living and preparing to battle the dark Sorceress. This worried her, but it did nothing to put an end to her reign of terror. Despite the rumors, there still weren't enough of us to do anything but watch and wait."

"What were you waiting for?"

"For the fulfillment of prophesy. For Fortis to return to Daak in its hour of greatest need," the magician answered. "We were waiting for you, Rodney."

"But I'm not Fortis."

The Ward's smile returned to the face of Archimagus. "We shall debate that later, but first let me answer a question that you have not yet asked. While it is true that Yens lied about why he brought you here, much of what he said was factual, including the part about me being the most powerful magician on Daak. You are no doubt wondering, then, why I am not able to defeat Haeron on my own."

"Why do you need us?"

"The reason is because my powers are based on white magic while hers are heavily based in black magic. White magic, you see, is not an aggressive art. We use it for healing, illusion and the sort. There are very few offensive spells that I have been able to master. Black magic, on the other hand, is primarily offensive. While the hated Sorceress is a mistress of her art, her ability to do useful, positive magic is almost nonexistent. However when it comes to the attack, to destruction, curses and plagues, her skill is consummate. If I were to pit my constructive power against her destructive I would be lucky to achieve a stalemate. Most likely the confrontation would lead to my death.

"But now that you are here, Rodney, all that has changed. Alone, neither of us could make much of a difference. Together we will defeat Haeron and restore peace to all of Daak."

Rodney was skeptical. "If you're the same Archimagus that really did fight with Fortis all those centuries ago, how can you still be alive and why do you look so young? Can white magic make you live forever?"

"White magic *can* extend your life for many, many years, as can black magic. It's a little like the principle of a battery that you told me about during your last visit to Daak. A true magician recharges his life forces with his magic. But magic can't make you live forever, and to tell you the truth I have no idea why I'm still alive. All I know is that I've barely aged since the day that I first met you."

"You keep saying that, but I know I've never met you before just the other day, and I never even heard of Fortis until I read about him in that book in Yens' library. Maybe you made a mistake and I just look like the Fortis you remember."

"I'm truly sorry if this causes you any confusion, but believe me, no one who has met Fortis could ever forget him. But as I'm the only person still alive who was around when Fortis lived and reigned among the Truculans, I guess you'll have to take my word for it. But aside from that, I know you are Fortis because I knew you before you became Fortis. When you first came to us those many centuries ago you had another name, but when you were taken into the Quabi'il tribe you were given a Quabi'ili name by my father who was the tribal leader. I was one of the few who knew Fortis' Earth name: Rodney Shuster of Auburn in the province of New York in the land called the United States of America. I know everything about you from our many talks when you first arrived to live among us."

"Prove it."

Archimagus grinned as he brought forth one of his favorite memories of the past. "Fortis' appetite is almost as legendary as his heroics, and there was one Truculan dish that you liked more than any other, a pastry made from the fruit of the byn tree. I remember one time when the two of us disobeyed a direct order from my father and raided the food stores of the neighboring Takka'il tribe to steal all their byn fruit to give to our tribal chef so he could make these pastries for us.'

"That doesn't prove anything. I've never even heard of the byn tree or its fruit."

"The reason we risked angering the Takka'ili by taking their byn was because the pastries tasted like your favorite food in the whole world – your father's banana cream pies."

Rodney's jaw dropped. Aimee's jaw dropped. Yens looked at the twins and then his jaw dropped as well because he could see that this was the truth and that Archimagus knew more about Rodney than even he did.

"You are confused. In time you will come to understand all that I have said," the magician continued, "but that time may not come to pass for several years. Until then, I must ask that you trust me when I tell you that you are Fortis, uniter of the Truculans, savior of Daak. This is your world, my lord, and it lives only through you in a way that even I, who has lived here for nearly three thousand years, can never understand.

"I know this has been a lot for you to absorb, but in your heart you know that I'm telling the truth." The magician opened his arms wide. "Together, the five of us must succeed where countless others have failed. We must defeat Haeron. But before we can do that we must first deal with a more immediate concern. The Wild Ones have no doubt left sentries in the Cave, so we can't go back the way we came. We have to find another way out of this mountain."

CHAPTER SIXTEEN
The Long Jump

The discovery of the tunnel system within the mountain was no coincidence. Archimagus knew about it and had arranged things so that Rodney would find the entrance. Archimagus himself had discovered the tunnel years ago when he had first gone into hiding from Haeron.

Unfortunately, the circumstances at the time had made it impossible for him to do more than a cursory exploration of the system and the cave was the only way in that he was aware of. The untimely attack of the Wild Ones had made it impossible for them to go back the way they had come. They had to find another way out. Archimagus led the way as they searched the tunnels, using his green magic glow to light their path as effectively as any spotlight or torch could.

"Shouldn't we try to recover the Crown of Fortis first?" Rodney questioned.

"The Crown was never here," Archimagus admitted. "It was all an illusion created by me to test Yens and Ho-Don, to see if there was any good in them. His own story, the one he told last night, gave me the idea. Yens passed the test. Ho-Don failed and paid for it with his life."

Aimee was horrified. "That means the earthquake and everything else was your doing? Some test. Rodney could have been killed."

"Not at all," the magician responded. "The crevice was an illusion as well. Had your brother actually lost his grip he wouldn't have fallen more than a foot or two. The pit may have looked bottomless, but believe me, I would never put Fortis in unnecessary jeopardy. He is this planet's last hope for salvation. He is also my friend."

Aimee wasn't sure whether to be relieved by this or angry that Archimagus had played games with them. There was one thing she knew for certain, though. She was as important as Rodney to this mission, maybe even more so. If it hadn't been for her there wouldn't even be a mission still. The men would have all been killed in the Dismal Forest. She decided to tell him so, but he spoke before she could get a single word out.

"I know what you are about to say, Aimee, and you are absolutely right. Fortis has returned in fulfillment of the prophesy that he himself handed down to us, but he will not be able to liberate this world alone. You, too, are needed if we are to succeed as are Gillian, myself and even Yens. It was no accident that you were brought here when Yens cast the spell Haeron had given him to transport Rodney to Daak. That was my doing. I was the Ward you saw in the playground in Foran Village as well. I have been monitoring your progress from the very beginning."

Archimagus paused and looked at Gillian. "It is also no accident that you are here with us," he admitted. "The fallen tree that forced us to stop in the Dismal Forest was my doing too, another one of my illusions. I also used my powers to misdirect your sisters in the forest to give us time to escape. Haeron will be defeated, but only if we all work together. Please forgive me if I sometimes speak only of Fortis. I've known him the longest but we are all integral parts of this operation."

Aimee nodded as they continued on in silence. It felt good to finally hear someone acknowledge her importance, even if she really didn't understand everything that was going on right now.

This new tunnel that they were on twisted and curved considerably more than the one that brought them down into the belly of the mountain, but it wasn't nearly as steep. They walked for quite a distance, but it seemed that they were going more in circles than up. They felt that they were making at least marginal progress, however, so they continued to push on. Presently, they began to hear something in the distance. It was very faint at first but quickly became louder until it was a deafening roar that ricocheted through the tunnel.

A couple of twists in the shaft and Archimagus' magical beacon was no longer needed. Enough outside light was filtering in to let them know that they would soon be out. There was also another clue.

"Water," Rodney said as he ran a finger across the rough stone wall. He had to shout to be heard over the noise.

"There'll be plenty more where that came from if my guess is right," Yens shouted back. "Walk carefully from here on out. It's bound to be slippery."

One last turn and the tunnel opened up to a cavern similar to the one that they had originally sought refuge in, but it didn't lead to the open air as they had hoped it would. A wall of plunging water stretched completely across the mouth of the cave obscuring any view of the landscape beyond. This was the source of the noise.

"It's beautiful," Aimee said as she stared at the sparkling effect created by light refracting through the wall. "We must have come out right behind the waterfall."

While his sister was taking in the view, Rodney crept to the lip of the mouth and looked over the ledge. "The mountain's worn smooth by all the water here and it doesn't look like there's any path down. We're going to have to go back and try to find another way out."

Yens stood next to him and studied the drop. "We can't waste time searching for an exit that may not even exist. We go down here."

"How?"

"We jump."

* * *

After a short discussion it was decided that they would wait until dusk before making the jump to minimize the possibility that any Wild Ones might be wandering down by the lake. This would also give them a few hours to find another, safer exit. Because there was no light source other than Archimagus' magic, they weren't able to split up and look in different directions. Yens and the girls elected to wait where they were while Rodney and the magician searched for another way out.

"I don't know, Archimagus," Rodney said after they had walked far enough to talk again without screaming. "It's kind of hard thinking of you as a great magician. You did such a good job pretending to be that stupid Ward."

"If I had revealed myself prematurely, Yens would have reported back to Haeron immediately and all would have been lost. I had to bide my time and act the part of the Ward so that the prophesy can be fulfilled. Even as we speak there are still thousands of people, the descendants of the original Truculans, playing the part of the Wards all over this world. They talk stupid and they act stupid, but they are wisely watching and waiting. When the word is given, their true natures will be revealed and the prophesy that you yourself gave us centuries ago will come to pass."

"Look, Archimagus…"

"Can I ask you a favor, Rodney?" the magician interrupted.

"What?"

"Would you please stop calling me Archimagus? It sounds long and stuffy. You used to just call me Archie."

"Why do you keep pretending that you know me? I don't mind calling you Archie now, but I never used to do it because I didn't know you until we met by the stream before entering the Dismal Forest, and even then I thought your name was Ward." Rodney removed the bow that was holstered across his back and held it up. "You may think I'm Fortis because Yens gave me this to carry, but I'm not. I'm only Rodney Shuster, a twelve-year-old boy who never did anything important in his life before coming to Daak."

Archie smiled the Ward's smile and glanced at the bow in the young boy's hands. "It was destiny, not mere coincidence, that you chose that particular weapon to carry, neither was it coincidence that it was designed for your exact size and strength. You are Fortis and all that I have said is true. As I told you earlier, you may not understand any of this now but you will someday. I promise."

Rodney grew quiet for a moment as he thought this over. He had many more questions to ask, but a soft rumble in the silence put his mind on other matters. "I'm hungry again," he said, patting his stomach.

Archie reached into one of his pockets and handed Rodney a couple strips of jerky that he had taken from one of Ho-Don's supply bags. "Let's not worry any more about the past or the future," he said as the boy eagerly accepted the dried meat and started chewing. "Right now we have enough to keep us occupied here in the present. We've got some preparations to make if we're going to rescue our horses from the Wild Ones without getting ourselves captured or killed. Come here. Let me show you a relatively simple magic trick that an old friend of mine once taught me."

Rodney moved closer and watched intently as Archimagus detailed the preparations for his spell.

* * *

"Is everyone clear on what we're about to do?"

Aimee looked over the ledge and stared at the point where the falling waters disappeared into the rising mists. A lump formed in her throat. "How do we know that there aren't any rocks down there?"

"We don't know for sure," Yens admitted, "but I don't remember seeing any when we were down there and Archimagus doesn't detect any with his magic. This should be about as safe as jumping off the side of a mountain can be."

"That's not very reassuring. I still think we'd be better off looking for another way out."

"There is no other way out," Archimagus said, joining the conversation. "I did a scan of the tunnels when Rodney and I went back down. I am positive now that there are only two exits, this one and the way we came in. The Wild Ones have left sentries behind to kill us if we go back the other way, which leaves this as our only option."

Yens paced around the cave impatiently. "We're wasting time. We need to jump now while there's still some light left to see by."

"What about the Wild Ones?"

"They'll be heading back to their camps to hide from the night and all it brings. Now is the perfect time to do this. Who wants to go first?"

"I will," Rodney said, swallowing hard. He had meant for his words to sound brave, but his voice betrayed him as it crackled and echoed with uncertainty. Before he could change his mind and chicken out, he ran to the mouth of the cave and jumped. His scream was drowned out by the roar of the rushing waters before his plummeting form disappeared into the spray.

Archimagus was the next to go. After waiting a couple of minutes to make sure that Rodney had time to swim out of the way below, he walked to the edge and looked down. Without ceremony he simply stepped off and let himself drop.

"You're next," Yens said to Aimee after Archimagus was out of sight.

"I don't think I can."

"You can because you have no choice. Now are you going to jump off yourself or will I have to pick you up and throw you over?"

"I'll do it myself," Aimee answered with a mixture of fear and indignation. She walked to the lip, stared at the swirling mists below and froze.

"You can do it, sister," Gillian encouraged as Aimee stood there motionless. "Everything will be fine. Airia herself will guide you safely down."

Aimee looked back and drew comfort from Gillian's smile. "Here goes nothing," she said. Closing her eyes and plugging her nose, she took a deep breath, said a quick, silent prayer and then flung herself off the mountain.

"Your turn," Yens told Gillian.

"No," she answered simply. "It's your turn. I won't be going."

"What do you mean?"

"Just what I said, I'm not going. You men are so dense. Now hurry and jump because the others are waiting for you."

"I don't understand."

Gillian looked down at the wet stone floor to avoid the older man's stare. "What's to understand? I grew up in the forest where you found me. There were no lakes or any other bodies of water deep enough that I could learn to swim. If I jump I will die for certain. My only chance for survival is to remain here and hope that eventually the Wild Ones will leave the cave so I can sneak out that way."

Yens shook his head. "You will starve to death before that happens. The Wild Ones are nothing if not relentless. You're staying with us." Quickly, without giving the girl a chance to resist, he scooped her up in his arms, ran to the mouth of the cave and jumped off.

Gillian tried to hold her breath but it was impossible. The helplessness of falling through the air was frightening, and despite her warrior training she found herself screaming. The drop seemed forever. They couldn't see exactly where the air ended and the water began because of the mists kicked up by the waterfall, so the sudden impact with the surface of the lake was a shock to both of them.

Gillian clutched Yens tighter when they hit. Panic started to set in. She was still screaming when they made contact with the lake and water flooded her lungs. The distance from the cave to the surface was considerable, and their momentum drove them down deep into the lake.

Gillian didn't think they would ever stop going down, away from the safety of the shore, away from the life-preserving air. Her lungs burned and she had to fight the instinct to breathe in. Any more water in her lungs would kill her. Closing her eyes, she tightened her grip on Yens but knew it was only a matter of time. She was out of oxygen and felt like her lungs were about to burst.

And still they sank, until Yens felt his feet hit something hard. The bottom of the lake. He was confused and disoriented, but he managed to kick off at an angle that he thought would take them away from the mountain and they were going up again. With his free arm he pushed furiously against the water, fighting to reach the surface. Gillian was no longer clinging to him. She had gone limp in his arms.

Yens surfaced right beneath the waterfall and was immediately pushed back under. Holding tight to Gillian's body with one hand he struggled to recover his bearings and swam as best he could with his other in what he prayed was a safe direction. When he surfaced the second time he was well away from the falls. Gasping for breath he took air deeply into his lungs. He was the only one breathing.

Looking around frantically, he discovered that he was not all that far from shore. Archie and Rodney were both resting safely on the beach while Aimee, wading ankle deep, was about to step out of the lake when she spun around and looked at the struggling Yens. Without a second thought she dove back into the water and swam to the man. Together they gently towed Gillian's body toward shore.

"She's not breathing," Yens said as he stared with disbelief at the unmoving body that they had just lowered to the sand. He looked over at Archie. "You're the magician. Do something. Save her."

Archimagus lowered his head. "I'm not God," he quietly answered. "As powerful as my magic may be, I don't have the ability to restore life to the dead. There is nothing that I can do."

"Maybe I can help," Rodney said in a nervous, uncertain voice. Dropping to his knees in the sand next to Gillian he pressed two of his fingers against her wrist. Satisfied that she still had a pulse he shifted to tilt her head back and then pinched her nostrils firmly together with those same two fingers. Then, after taking a deep breath, he placed his lips over Gillian's and exhaled. Nothing happened.

Tears formed in Rodney's eyes but he didn't give up. Three, four more times he force air into Gillian's mouth. He bent over to do so a fifth time when he heard a faint noise. It was barely audible at first, but grew louder with each recurrence. Gillian was breathing. With Archie's help, Rodney turned her on her side. She was shaking uncontrollably and coughing up water, but she was very much alive.

Yens gaped at Rodney. "You have breathed life into the dead. When Haeron bade me to bring you into Daak she didn't tell me that you wielded such potent magic. Surely your power must rival her own."

"I'm no magician," Rodney said, rubbing his face with his hands in a futile attempt to hide the fact that he had been crying. "What I did was called mouth-to-mouth resuscitation and there was nothing mystical about it. It's easy to do and anyone can be taught how. I learned it when I was on the swim team in school."

"Then you must teach it to me when we get the chance. Magic or not, it seems to be a valuable skill that everyone should possess."

"Indeed," Archimagus agreed. "I, too, would be interested in learning how, but that will have to wait for another time. Right now there is a bit of my own magic that I would like to show you. It may not be as important as what Rodney just did, but I think you'll like it." Without saying another word, he began gathering up stones and placing them in a pile near where Gillian was resting. The twins looked on in curiosity, but the magician continued about his work in silence until he had collected a neat group of stones in a circular pile about two feet across.

"What's that for?" Aimee wanted to know.

Archimagus looked up at the quickly darkening western sky and then over to Aimee. "Gillian is in no condition to move and won't be for a couple of hours at least. We're soaked and the night air is chilly. We need to dry off and gather our strength before we can consider doing anything else."

"That makes sense," Aimee admitted as she pointed to the pile that he had gathered, "but I don't see how these rocks are going to help us do that."

In way of an answer Archie stuck his hands out and held them palms down over the pile. Closing his eyes in concentration, he muttered strange unintelligible sounds that were barely audible beneath his even breath. He continued like that in a trance-like state for several moments, but nothing seemed to happen. Then Aimee jumped back in surprise. The rocks were getting hot.

"That should do it," Archie said when the stones were glowing red. He stepped back to observe his handiwork. "What we need to do now is rest up and dry off. It's dark enough that the Wild Ones should be hiding in the safety of their camps, but I'll stand watch just in case. Why doesn't everyone else try to catch a little sleep."

The twins didn't have to be told twice. The jump had taken something out of each of them. They huddled around the rocks near where Gillian was already fast asleep, embracing the heat. Even Yens laid down without an argument and closed his eyes. Within minutes, Archimagus was the only one still awake.

CHAPTER SEVENTEEN
Heavenfall

It was a beautiful night and Daak's two moons shone brilliantly in the foreground of a star-packed sky. Archie stared patiently at the heavens for several hours as the others slept. Around midnight a small but bright light flickered across the sky before burning itself out over the eastern horizon. No sooner had it faded from sight than a second one appeared and followed a path similar to the first. It, too, died low in the eastern sky just moments before a third light began its flight. Archimagus rose to his feet. With a wave of his hand he bathed the area with his green magical light.

It was time.

Making his rounds, he woke everyone up, starting with Yens and finishing with Gillian. "How are you?" he asked as he carefully shook the young girl.

Gillian slowly opened her eyes. When she was able to focus them she saw four concerned faces looking down at her. "What happened?"

"You took in a large amount of water," Yens explained as he patted Rodney on the back. "We thought we were going to lose you, but our young friend here took control and saved your life."

Rodney started to turn away to hide his blushing, but a small hand reached up and stopped him. "Thank you," Gillian whispered softly.

Rodney opened his mouth but no words came out. He looked down at her smiling face and for the first time noticed just how soft and pretty her features were. The evening sky mirrored in her big brown eyes, and Rodney felt himself getting lost as he stared into them. Enjoying the feeling, he watched the reflected stars twinkle for several seconds until one of them began to slide across her eyes. His head snapped up just in time to see it fade away into the east.

"It started about ten minutes ago," Archimagus explained. "There can be no better night to do this."

"Why?" Asked Aimee.

A twin pair of lights rocketed across the sky and Archimagus watched them fade into oblivion. "I suppose we have time," he said. "This should last another hour or two."

The magician picked out a comfortable spot and sat on the ground near the glowing rocks. He waited for everyone to follow his lead before continuing. "What's happening in the skies above us is nothing more than a meteor storm. Rocks traveling through space come into contact with Daak's atmosphere and burn up from friction before they can hit the ground. What we see is the light they give off as they burn. The same thing happens on your Earth, but from what I understand a lot less frequently than it does here on Daak."

"I know all about meteor storms from science class," Aimee told him. "I meant, why is there no better time than now to rescue our horses?"

"Like many people on Daak, the Wild Ones are very superstitious. They don't understand what causes the meteor storm so therefore they fear it. They call it Heavenfall."

"You used that word when we first came to Daak," Rodney pointed out as he looked over to Yens.

Yenspetsnicksnack shrugged his shoulders. "This talk of burning rocks is new to me, but I am very interested. Please continue, magician."

"With pleasure, but first I have a question for you. Do you know the legend behind the first Heavenfall?"

Yens admitted that he didn't.

"Very well, then that is where I shall start for I know the story well. I was a part of it. In fact, you might say that I'm responsible for it." Archie took a deep breath. "The Wild Ones weren't always the savage and uncivilized creatures we just encountered. Centuries ago they were part of a peaceful race known as the Pacatus who lived in Blossom Valley in a province far to the south of here.

"The Pacatus were ruled by a wise and caring man, King Selyx, under whom they grew and prospered. They developed a trading arrangement with the men and women of the hills that overlooked Blossom Valley, an arrangement that benefited both peoples. The Hill People would send down products that they had mined from the ground and lumber that they had harvested from the trees that grew in abundance on their land. The Pacatus, in return, would send us fruits and vegetables grown in the fertile valley soil and fish caught in the river that ran through their territory.

"They say that all good things must come to an end, and for the Pacatus the end almost began when King Selyx died. The only heir to the throne, Prince Mal, was neither as wise nor as peace loving as his father. Mal was a foolish and greedy man. He envied the Hill People for their vast resources and became quite selfish with the resources of the valley. Essentially, he wanted everything that the Hill People had but didn't want to give up anything of his own. Puum, the king of the Hill People, was young and did not yet have an heir, so Mal reasoned that if Puum were to die without a descendant, the Hill People would turn to Mal to rule them. He would then have all the combined wealth of both peoples for himself.

"To achieve Puum's death, Mal set up a party to trap him. He sent a messenger to the people of the hills and invited their leaders to a massive celebration that would culminate with Mal's coronation. Although Prince Mal had his supporters, the majority of Pacatus enjoyed their friendship with the Hill People. They would have been appalled if they knew what Mal was planning so he had to be careful to keep his plan a secret from his own people as well as those of the hills.

"His plan would probably have worked except for the fact that a lowly page happened to overhear a conversation between Mal and two of his loyal servants as they discussed the murder of the king of the Hill People. This page described in detail what he had heard to Wylsun, who had been the advisor and friend of King Selyx and was just as wise as the late monarch had been. Wylsun, in turn, sent a second messenger into the hills to warn Puum of Mal's evil plan.

"Now, Puum wasn't the brightest man who ever lived, but he had a heart of gold and was as loved by his people as Selyx had been by the Pacatus. Worried that he couldn't handle the situation himself, he sent a messenger to Sedes to enlist my aid. Naturally, I went right away."

Archimagus paused to contemplate the star-laden sky. Three separate meteor flares told him that the storm was still going strong and he continued. "To shorten this story, the coronation went as planned, and as far as Mal knew Puum arrived at the celebration as expected."

"I don't understand," Aimee interrupted. "If Puum knew that Mal wanted to kill him, why did he go to the coronation?"

"Let me finish and I'll tell you. Like I said, *as far as Mal knew,* Puum went to the celebration. In reality, Puum was still safely hidden away up in the hills. I had used my magic to create an animated likeness of him, and it was this likeness that Mal greeted. It was this likeness that was given a room in the royal palace for the night and it was this likeness that was 'killed' by Mal's assassins while it 'slept'. The next morning Mal claimed that thieves had stolen into the palace in the middle of the night and killed Puum. Mal sent word of this to the Hill People with his regrets, offering them his interim service as ruler. At this time, only Puum and myself knew that the king of the Hill People was still very much alive.

"Three days later it was announced that another ceremony was going to take place. Just as he had hoped, since there was no heir to succeed to Puum's throne, the Hill People were willing to unite with the Pacatus and crown Mal their king. The night of the ceremony came, and it was a night much like this one. By the time Mal was to be appointed, meteors were streaking across the sky in twos and threes. Science was a fledgling art in those days and beyond the Truculan border it was unheard of. I knew what the meteors were, but I was the only one who did. I decided to use that to my advantage.

"In the midst of the storm, just before Mal was to accept the crown of the Hill People, Puum and I appeared before the gathered masses. I told them of Mal's treachery, but in my zeal to impress upon everyone how evil he was, and in attempt to put righteousness on my side, I, well, I embellished the facts somewhat. Instead of telling them the truth, I told them that Mal had indeed succeeded in killing Puum and it was only through the grace and power of Feroxx that he was there with them now."

"You mean you lied."

"I was young then, barely two hundred years old. I had dramatic urges." Archie took a deep breath and watched another meteor meet its end in the east. "Yes, I lied. And once I started, there was no stopping me. I compounded one lie on top of another. Like I said, I knew even then that they were just rocks burning up from friction, but instead of educating the people I decided to feed on their superstitions. If I knew that today, centuries later, people would still believe my lies as truth I might not have said what I did, but I was too mired in the moment to think of the future. My lies were rooted firmly in the present, in that night.

"I told the crowd that each shooting star above was the flaming soul of a good person who in some way had been wronged while alive, burning with a thirst for vengeance. I said that they were being sent back to Daak by Feroxx to be given the opportunity to exact vengeance on the person or persons who had wronged them. That, I explained, was how Puum was able to stand alive before them. Nobody but Puum and myself knew the truth, and as far as I now, for as long as he lived, Puum never told anyone otherwise.

"But be that as it may, the people believed me and, to use an expression from your Earth, 'the end justified the means'. Mal was exposed as the evil man that he was and he and his supporters were driven out by the combined masses of the hills and the valley. Word of what he had done spread fast, and the supporters of Mal were forced to become nomadic wanderers for no people would take them in. The Wild Ones are their descendants."

"What happened to Puum?"

Archie answered with a smile. "It's actually very ironic. Mal's dream of uniting the Pacatus and the Hill People became a reality that night. With Mal driven away there was no heir to the Pacatus throne, so the people of Blossom Valley invited Puum to rule over them. This proved to be a very wise move and the combined peoples lived in peace and comfort for centuries. If it weren't for Haeron they would probably still be just as happy now, but the southern provinces were the first to fall. Today the children of Blossom Valley are slaves of the evil sorceress, forced by her greed to plunder the resources of their land. If they are ever to regain their peaceful home, if the people of Daak are ever to be free again, we must succeed in defeating Haeron."

"Then let's do it," Rodney said, jumping to his feet. "Let's go take our horses back and do it."

Inspired by the boy's enthusiasm, everyone else rose. Gillian was still exhausted from her ordeal, so she was the slowest to move. She held up an arm in Rodney's direction and he took hold of her hand to help pull her to her feet. When she was finally standing, Rodney noticed that she still had a firm grip on his hand. His first instinct was to pull his hand away, but he silently admonished himself for even thinking such a thing. This was the first time that Gillian had reached out to anyone other than Aimee for support. Besides, he had to admit, it kind of felt good holding her hand. Giving it a friendly squeeze, he shifted to look at her. This time he saw himself reflected in her eyes. "You okay?"

A smile grew on her face, but Rodney got the uneasy feeling that she was using it to mask her pain. "I'll make it," she whispered.

"Then let's get ready to move out,' Yens said, once more taking command. At his direction they gathered up those precious few supplies that they had managed to keep with them and started walking. They had surfaced not far from where they had abandoned the horses on the previous night when they were driven up into the mountain, so Yens and Archimagus reasoned that the horses would probably be in the nearest camp.

"That is," Yens reminded the group, "if the Wild Ones haven't eaten them yet."

Everyone shuddered at the thought, and Yens led them away from the lake. He took them up the highest of the nearby hills and from there they were able to see several small fires burning in the distance. Yens pointed to the closest one and they headed toward it, Archie's magical glow illuminating their path.

"Shouldn't you put the light out now?" Aimee asked. "If we can see their campfire, then it only makes sense to think that they are able to see our light too."

Archie pointed to the sky. "The whole point of what I just told you was that several centuries ago I made up a story about Heavenfall. I'm not proud of the fact that I lied, but after all these years that lie is going to work for us again. The Wild Ones fear the walk of the dead. They believe that the meteors above are souls being sent down to exact revenge upon their wrongdoers. Wild Ones aren't known for their ability to reason. They know what they see and they don't try to think past it. If we sneak into their camp like thieves, they will believe us to be thieves and will deal with us accordingly. If we march in looking like the resurrected dead, they will think we are the dead and will leave us alone, afraid that we might send them to Suroxx. At least that is what I hope will happen. I want to be seen."

Aimee accepted this explanation, and the group walked on in silence. Yens took the point, with Archie and his mystical light right behind him. Rodney and Gillian walked next, still hand in hand, and Aimee brought up the rear feeling like a fifth wheel.

They continued on like this for about thirty minutes until they were almost to the encampment. Archie stopped the group just before the last hill separating them from the camp. "You three wait here," he said, pointing to Yens and the girls. "It will be best if Rodney and I go the rest of the way alone. We'll get the horses and meet you back here."

"That's foolish," Yens argued. "If this trick doesn't work, if they even suspect that you are alive, you won't be for long. They will kill you in no time. You need us there as back-up."

Archimagus shook his head. "If this trick doesn't work, whoever goes into that camp will be killed, whether it's just me and Rodney or all five of us. Either this plan will work or it won't. We will emerge unscathed or be killed, there is no middle ground. At least my way we'll only be putting two of us at risk."

"Then let me go instead of Rodney. I am older, more experienced and I owe him my life. I can't hide in safety while Rodney puts himself in jeopardy."

Archie smiled and reached up to touch Yens on the shoulder. "Aimee was right. Yours are not the words of a coward. Nevertheless, you can and will stay here." Snapping off a twig from a nearby tree, he studied it approvingly. "Your time will not be wasted. This is a Vertee tree. Its branches grow straight and strong. While we are gone, you can use it to replenish the supply of arrows that were used fighting the Wild Ones in the cave."

"The children can do that. If anyone risks his life in the Wild One camp with you, it should be me."

Archie shook his head. "Show him why you're the best candidate for this mission, Rodney. Let him see what I taught you in the cave."

Rodney closed his eyes and took a deep breath. His brow wrinkled in concentration. When he reopened his eyes he was floating vertically about a foot in the air. "There," he said as he let the air back out of his lungs. "I did it." His face glowed with the proud look of accomplishment.

Archie waved a hand and as quickly as that he joined Rodney in levitation. "If the Wild Ones harbor any doubts about us, they should be dispelled when Rodney and I enter their camp literally walking on air. It has to be just the two of us."

Yens forced himself to smile and put a friendly hand on top of Rodney's head. "You better come back alive, boy," he said as he gently mussed Rodney's hair, "because when this is all over I plan to throw the biggest feast that Daak has ever seen and you're the only one with an appetite big enough to keep up with me."

It was an appealing offer, but Rodney, still angry over Yens' intended betrayal, shrank from the man's touch. "Let's get going, Archie," he said, deliberately turning his back on the mayor of Foran village.

* * *

In direct contrast to the permanence of the Sisterhood's village, the camp of the Wild Ones had a transitory look to it. This was to be expected. The Wild Ones were, after all, a nomadic people who lived off the land, hunting and foraging to survive. When the game left, they followed. When they had consumed all the fruits and berries in an area they moved their camp to where they could find more. The entire camp was portable, little more than a collection of stretched animal-hide tents centered around a common fire. The Wild Ones had very few possessions, only what they needed to survive. Anything else would encumber them when it came time to move on.

With Yens and the girls working on arrows back in the safety of the darkness, Rodney and Archimagus approached the camp. Rodney was still a little unsure of himself but in the short time he had known the sorcerer, both as Ward and Archimagus, he had grown to trust him. When the pair crossed the outer perimeter Rodney followed without hesitation. Still walking about a foot above the ground, still bathed in the mystical green light, the pair strolled boldly into the camp.

They looked around the encampment. With the exception of a trio of dogs that kept a respectful distance, and a fire that was left burning, there was no sign of any life at all.

"Where are the horses?"

Archie slowly scanned the area. "They're here," he said with assurance. "As are the Wild Ones, so we'd better maintain the act."

"What do you mean?"

Archimagus directed his answer to the entire camp. "Listen to me, cowards. You took our lives and our horses, not in battle but through treachery and shame," he shouted, pointing to the skies above, still being lit up by the falling stars. "But by the grace of Feroxx and the glory that is Heavenfall we have been allowed to come back and exact vengeance. We shall be satisfied with our horses, but let it be known that anyone who tries to stop us shall be smote down and condemned to spend eternity in the cold, damning grip of Suroxx."

Slowly, dramatically, Archimagus lifted his arms high above his head. His words became strange, unrecognizable sounds that he now muttered quietly under his breath.

The wind began to blow, swirling and eddying in the gaps between the tents. Soon the wind was whistling all about them with an almost tornado-like intensity, whipping at the edges of the tents and threatening variably to spread and extinguish the fire. Now, Archie was shouting. Now the wind screamed all about them. With a sudden gust the fire was gone, leaving Archie's glow the only remaining light.

Rodney stood dumbfounded as he watched the wind pound at the stretched animal hides. Standing by Archie's side, he was completely untouched by the wind, safe in the eye of the hurricane. Meteors danced across the sky above, living and dying with a fury that echoed that of the storm below.

Suddenly one of the tents popped off its mountings, soaring into the air and out of the range of Archie's light, exposing its inhabitants to the winds. A second stretched skin took flight, followed by a third and then a fourth until, very quickly, there were no tents left in camp. Most, like the first, revealed small groups of Wild Ones clustered together with fear, but the largest and last was hiding the missing horses.

Archie lowered his arms and as quickly as it had begun the wind stopped. The Wild Ones, ugly, hairy and huge, stared dumbly at them. Rodney was frightened, but it was obvious that he and Archie were having an even greater effect on them. He had to resist two conflicting urges. Part of him wanted to break into a panicked run while another part of him wanted to march right up to the nearest cluster and really give them a scare. He settled for the middle ground and waited to follow Archie's lead. He didn't have long to wait. Before either of them could do anything, the Wild Ones began to back off slowly, disappearing one by one into the night. The dogs quickly followed their masters, and in a matter of heartbeats the savages were all gone. Archie and Rodney were left alone with the horses.

"Let's not press our luck," Archimagus suggested. "We would be wise to grab the horses and get out of here before the Wild Ones find their courage and return to confront us."

By the time Archie had finished speaking Rodney was already wrapping his arms around Credalis' neck, greeting his trusted mount with a hug.

CHAPTER EIGHTEEN
Betrayal

Archie's theatrics were effective. The Wild Ones had fled the area in fear and it was now a simple matter to lead the horses over the hill to where Yens and the girls were waiting. Aimee cried when she saw Ed, throwing her arms around his neck and hugging him for all he was worth.

"It doesn't look good," Yens said as he dug through the saddlebags. "The Wild Ones ate what little food we had left. Fortunately, they didn't take this." He withdrew a large crystal and admired it.

"What is it?"

Yens glanced down at the ground and then back at the crystal. "This is the device I used to communicate with Haeron to inform her of our progress. When the time is right I will contact her with it one last time." With great care he placed it gently in the saddlebag and changed the subject. "But at the moment we have other concerns. We need to get as far away from here as possible before the Wild Ones gather reinforcements and come looking for us."

With Ho-Don gone, Gillian was able to ride the extra packhorse. She needed a minimal amount of instruction, which Rodney was all too eager to provide, and soon she was adequately prepared to ride on her own. Travel was slow because both moons had set and they were left with only the glow of Archie's magic to see by. Still, thanks to the show that he had put on while retrieving the horses, they were able to travel without incident and by sunrise they were miles from the nearest Wild One camp.

They stopped by a stream on the edge of the Dismal Forest and breakfasted on some berries that Yens found. As their riders ate, the horses drank from the brook and ate the lush grass that grew alongside it.

"It's beautiful here," Aimee said. Her stomach was full and she leaned against a nearby tree with her eyes only half open. She watched a pair of butterflies dart playfully around a colorful patch of wild flowers. Every hill for as far as she could see was graced with banks of these gorgeous flowers and a gentle breeze seemed to exist only to deliver their sweet scents to Aimee's nose. Birds more lovely than any she had ever seen fluttered over and around the sprawling hills, landing in the occasional tree and filling the air with their rich songs.

"It sure is beautiful," Yens agreed quickly. "Beautiful and restful. The way I see it, even with the time lost to the Sisterhood and the Wild Ones, we're still at least a day ahead of schedule because we found Archimagus without having to cross the Barrier Mountains. We've been through quite a lot. Why don't we take a day to rest? We won't do anything but relax and enjoy the beauty that surrounds us."

No one argued with him, and soon Yens was standing guard while the others slept in the morning sun. Despite his best efforts to stay alert, however, he too quickly fell asleep. Fortunately, they were far enough away from any potential trouble that their slumber went undisturbed. It was about midday before the first of them stirred, and soon they were all awake and sitting in the shade of a cluster of trees.

"I'm hungry again," Rodney announced, and his belly rumbled to stress the point.

"There are plenty of berries left."

The boy wrinkled his nose. "I want something more filling. Are you sure that the Wild Ones ate all our food?"

Yens nodded. "Every last bite. There wasn't so much as a crumb left in the bags. I'm afraid it's berries or nothing."

"I'm a warrior," Gillian reminded them, not for the first time. She pointed toward the edge of the forest with her bow. "There is no way in imagination that I'm going to eat berries when there is game nearby. I crave fresh meat. I'm sure I can hunt us up something in there."

"Out of the question," Yens answered. "It's far too dangerous. You could get lost in there or worse. We don't really know where we are or what might be around. We're safer if we all stay together right here."

"And we'd be even safer if you had stayed at home and never begun this quest," Gillian snapped. "I'd still be with my sisters and you would all be comfortable in your own homes. Airia teaches us that one cannot live unless one is willing to take risks, but going into the forest will not be a risk for me. I grew up there and I'm not going to lose my way. You go ahead and eat your berries now, but we will eat a supper fit for warriors because I am going hunting. Does anyone wish to join me?"

Rodney jumped to his feet and pulled his quiver and bow from Credalis' pack. The quiver was once again full of arrows. "I'm with you," he proudly announced, as if daring Yens to say anything more. When he didn't the two of them walked side-by-side toward the forest. Rodney waited until they were out of earshot of the others before adding, "but just in case it takes us a while to get anything, I pocketed a handful of berries."

* * *

"How come you didn't go with them?" Archie asked as he watched Rodney and Gillian disappear into the forest. Yens, at the same time, was heading toward the berry bushes in almost the exact opposite direction.

Aimee shrugged her shoulders and a shock of blonde hair fell over her eyes. "I don't know," she answered as she patted the curl back into place. Her eyes were focused on the ground. "I'd probably just end up getting in the way.'

"You sound a little jealous," the magician pointed out.

Aimee lifted her eyes. "Maybe," she said with another shrug. "It's just not fair. Gillian was my friend first, and now all of a sudden she's best buddies with Rodney and ignoring me. Two days ago she hated all men and wanted to kill him. In fact, I thought she was going to when he stole our clothes while we were swimming, and now they're acting like they've been friends forever. I don't understand it."

"If you will remember, at the same time he was stealing Gillian's clothes, I was right there stealing yours and yet we're both here able to have a mature and friendly conversation."

"Well, yeah, but that's different. You were just pretending to be a stupid Ward then but now you're Archimagus, the planet's greatest magician. Rodney's still just my dumb brother."

"If there is one thing I've learned after all these centuries, it's that people and things change." Archie popped a berry in his mouth and chewed it. "Besides, even though it's sometimes hard to see how at first, change often occurs for the better, and I think this is one of those times. When we first met Gillian she hated all men no matter what. She's only been with us for a couple of days but already she is learning that it's important to judge people by what's inside, not what they look like on the outside. Just because she is finally accepting Rodney as a friend doesn't mean that she's excluding you. I'll bet there's plenty of room in her heart for both of you."

"Do you really think so?"

"I know so," Archie answered with a warm smile. "You don't get to be as old as I am without learning how to read people."

Aimee smiled back. "Change must be a good thing because I like you a lot better now that you've changed into Archimagus. Thank you."

"My pleasure, but right now we need to set our mind on other matters. Haeron's castle lies in Bear Swamp to the east of the Dismal Forest, about two day's ride from here. As soon as Yens gets back we'll need to make plans for our final assault. Care to join us?"

"Me?" Aimee asked, beaming.

"You orchestrated our escape from the Sisterhood of Airia, and you will play a crucial role in the final battle. I think it's important that you have a say in our final plans."

* * *

The fire writhed and flickered from within the confines of the stone-bordered pit, spitting its glow unevenly at Aimee, Yens and Archimagus. A thick bank of clouds obscured the twin domains of Suroxx above, preventing any additional light from filtering down.

"I knew I should have been more insistent about not letting them go," Yens said, admonishing himself. "There's no way they'll ever find their way back now, not without the light of the moons to guide them."

"Have faith in the abilities of a warrior, man," a voice called out from the darkness. Gillian and Rodney stepped into range of the fire, a small boar dangling from a stick between them. "Tonight we feast."

Gillian had already dressed and skinned the boar where she had dropped it, so it was a simple matter to prepare it for cooking. Yens rigged up a makeshift spit, and it wasn't too terribly long before they were dining on pork. Soon after that the children, full and content, were all fast asleep despite Archie's eagerness to tell them some of the stories he had heard or experienced during his many centuries of life. Yens and

Archie split the night into two watches, and the evening passed without incident into the next day.

The ride that morning was as uneventful as the night had been, and lunchtime saw the end of both the berries and the pork. "We'll find something for dinner," Yens said, trying to reassure Rodney who was practically in tears when the last of the food had been eaten.

They mounted back up and continued east toward Haeron's castle. The sun was warm but not too hot and a fresh breeze played with their faces as they rode along the edge of the Dismal Forest. Soon the forest bent south and they maintained their easterly course leaving the woods far behind.

About an hour before sundown they passed a small stream and Yens decided to stop for the day to give them time to find something for dinner while there was still light. At his command they dismounted and led the horses to the water.

The horses weren't the only ones thirsty. Because they had been forced to abandon almost everything while fleeing the Sisterhood, they no longer had their canteens with them, and this was the first water they had found since stopping for lunch several hours ago.

Yens, Archie and the girls bent down by the stream and cupped water with the palms of their hands to drink. Rodney, more impatient than the others, waded into the middle of the brook and plunged his head right into the water to gulp at it. When he pulled his head back out he was startled to see what the others had already noticed. They were completely surrounded by a large group of men dressed entirely in animal skins. Each of the men held a sword pointed at the travelers, and they all wore some kind of war paint on their faces. "We're not looking for trouble," Yens was telling them. "Just let us get to our horses and we'll move on."

The strangers continued to stare and point their swords, but they remained silent.

Reaching behind her, Aimee pulled out her bow and placed a single arrow against its string.

"Don't be foolish," Yens said when he saw what she was doing. "There have to be at least fifty of them. We won't stand a chance if we start a fight. Our only hope is to try and find some way to reason with them."

"Trust me," Aimee told him as she pointed the arrow at the men. "I know what I'm doing." She studied the paint on their faces, settled on one of the men, took aim and fired her arrow. It fell short, embedding in the dirt just inches from his feet.

Instantly, the man drew his sword back and flung it. It sliced through the air before cleaving deep in the bank right next to Aimee. Everyone jumped when the sword was thrown. Everyone, that is, except for Aimee. She simply pulled it back out of the ground, walked toward the man who had chucked it, and handed it back to him hilt first. He, in turn, handed Aimee's arrow back to her.

"These are the Salltus," she explained to her friends as she accepted her arrow back. "I recognized them from their clothing and facial paint. They are nomads, like the Wild Ones, but are a civilized people if you know how to greet them. I identified the leader from the patterns of his war paint and initiated the disarmament ceremony. By firing my arrow in the ground, I was showing them that we don't want to fight and their leader offered me the same peace gesture by throwing his sword to me. We are now friends. If I hadn't been willing to part with my arrow they would have assumed us to be hostile and we would probably be dead right now."

Rodney's jaw dropped. "How could you possibly have known all that?"

Aimee shrugged her shoulders. "Simple. I did what I was supposed to do when we were in Yens' library. "I studied the books instead of rolling up in a ball and going to sleep. There was an entire chapter about the Salltus in one of the books Yens gave us to read."

"I am impressed," Yens told her. "Even I have never heard of these people, and I thought I had read every book in my study. I remember telling you both that learning what was in those books might mean the difference between life and death. Thank God at least one of you took me seriously. You have done well, Aimee."

It turned out that the Salltus were as accommodating to their friends as they were ruthless to their enemies, and Aimee's action did more than just save their lives. It also bought them a tasty and nutritious meal, hot baths and comfortable beds to spend the night in. After dinner a troop of Salltus dancers entertained them, but the travelers were too tired to fully appreciate all this and they all chose to turn in early. Well, all of them but one. Yens decided to stay up a little while longer.

* * *

"What is it?" the horrible voice demanded. "How dare you disturb me this late at night?"

"My apologies, great Haeron," Yens said humbly into the crystal, "but I had to make sure that the others were fast asleep before I contacted you."

"This had better be good news."

"It is, my liege, it most certainly is. We will reach your castle in a couple of days. Archimagus and the children still have no clue where my loyalty truly lies, and by the time they figure it out I will have enslaved them. Their helpless bodies will be delivered to you and my task will be done."

"And the hidden city of the Truculans?"

"There is no hidden city, Great Haeron. It exists only in the forsaken dreams of those you have conquered."

"It makes no difference, lord governor," Haeron cackled. "You have succeeded in the most important part of your mission, the capture of Archimagus. You will be greatly rewarded for your efforts."

CHAPTER NINETEEN
Haeron

"What is going on?"

Galen winced. He had been chief advisor to the morbid sorceress long enough to know her moods, and from the tone in her voice she was anything but happy. The more irritated she became the more prone to violence she would be, and he didn't plan to make himself an easy target. "The first of them arrived late last night, your majesty, and they have been coming steadily ever since. Latest estimate says there are about three thousand of them, quite possibly every one on the entire planet."

"And what are they doing?"

"Playing."

"Playing?"

"Yes, my liege, playing. Scouts have reported that they are playing all sorts of games from hopscotch to kickball to several that our soldiers have never heard of."

Haeron squinted as she surveyed the situation from her balcony. She couldn't think of anything she hated more than a Ward, and here there were thousands of them infesting the lawns outside her castle playing their stupid games.

"Orders your highness?"

Haeron looked at Galen with contempt. He was a spineless worm, yet he served a purpose. He was just about the only one of her servants she could trust completely, and if she gave him an instruction she knew it would be carried out. "Ignore them for the time being and continue preparing for the feast. I'll waste neither manpower nor ammunition on the likes of their stupidity unless I have no other choice. Has there been any word yet from that fool Yenspetsnicksnack?"

"The mayor of Foran Village was sighted by a slaving patrol early this morning," Galen meekly responded. "They reported that he had Archimagus and the boy in chains but stated that there was no sign of either of the girls. He should be arriving with his prisoners at any time now. Do you wish me to establish contact with him?"

Haeron opened her mouth, but a high-pitched beep from a nearby table distracted her before she could answer. "Speak of the maggot," she said as she looked over to the communication crystal glowing only a couple of feet away. "It appears that he is contacting me. Leave."

"Yes, your majesty," Galen answered. Bowing low, he backed his way out of the room as quickly as he could without making it look like he was anxious to get away from her.

Haeron slammed the door as he left and then walked over to the crystal. Pushing a button to activate it, she watched as Yens' head flickered into focus. A small gash on his forehead had been hastily bandaged, but it was still oozing a little blood. The dark sorceress glared at the image in the orb. "Report."

"Greetings, your eminence. My apologies for not contacting you sooner."

"Forget the amenities and get straight to your report," Haeron snapped.

"As you wish, my liege. Last night, as the others slept, I managed to slip the magical handcuffs that you had given me onto Archimagus. They worked just as you had promised they would and rendered him completely powerless. I also managed to incapacitate Rodney without incident.

"The girls, however, heard me coming and put up a struggle. As you can see, I was injured in the fight. I know you wanted me to bring them all in alive, but please believe me that I had no other choice. The girls both fled. When I was unable to capture them I did the only other thing possible. I shot them in the back as they ran away. I was afraid that if I allowed them to live they might try to rescue the other two and delay my delivering Archimagus to you. I hope you are not upset with your humble servant, great Haeron."

The cruel sorceress mulled this over for a second. "You have acted properly, my lord governor," she finally said. Haeron tried to force a pleasant smile to her face, but it had been so long since she had grinned that all she was able to produce was a kind of crooked frown. "How long will it be until you are able to bring the boy and the magician to me?"

"If all goes well and your soldiers don't harass us, we shall be at the gates of your castle before nightfall."

CHAPTER TWENTY
The Black Castle

Haeron arranged for a squad of soldiers to meet Yens halfway and escort him back to her. As they neared the castle they had to wade through an endless sea of Wards to get to the entrance. The Wards, for their part, seemed to pay no attention to the procession. They simply parted to let the riders through and then resumed their games the moment the horses were past.

Evening was beginning to steal away the day and the black castle towered ominously in the late afternoon sun. As if in defiance of the landscape, it stood several meters higher than the tallest tree. Stone gargoyles stared down from their perches on every battlement, keeping silent watch on the Wards playing in the fields. Above them, guards paced back and forth on the parapet, carefully monitoring all traffic in and out of the fortress.

A thick, soupy moat circled the castle and the only way inside was across the lone drawbridge that at the moment was up, effectively keeping all intruders out and imprisoning its inhabitants within. A dirt rub, where the grass had been scraped clean from thousands of lowerings and raisings, marked where the bridge rested when down. The group was escorted to that point and ordered to wait. Having carried out their orders to deliver Yens and the prisoners to Haeron's doorstep, the soldiers make a hasty retreat lest their dark mistress be displeased for whatever reason and take her displeasure out on them.

"Traitor," Rodney spat at Yens as they waited for something to happen. The five horses, two of them without riders now, stood motionless despite the outburst.

"I did what I had to do. There is nothing you could have given me that Haeron cannot grant threefold. With the two of you safely under her control there is no one left with the power to challenge her, and she will owe her dominance solely to me. Her gratitude will know no bounds."

A loud wooden creak followed by the rattling of heavy chains filled the air as the drawbridge slowly dropped. Yens urged the horses across and into the courtyard of the castle.

"My lord governor," Haeron said, arms outstretched, as the group approached. "You have done well and I am pleased."

Yenspetsnicksnack slid off his mount and knelt as low as he could in front of her. "The mere knowing that I have pleased you brings me great pleasure in return, my queen."

Ignoring his groveling, Haeron stepped past Yens and paused before Archimagus. "What is this treachery?" she demanded as she gazed upon the magician's youthful face. "Archimagus is centuries old. You have brought me a mere pup." Haeron was infuriated and vented her anger on Yens with a strong backhand across the face, knocking him to the ground.

"Allow me to explain, Mistress," Yens pleaded as he rubbed the spot where Haeron had struck him. He tried to stand, but the evil sorceress slapped him right back down. This time he remained on the ground.

"You were saying, worm?"

Yens tried to look as dignified as possible on the ground. "This is indeed Archimagus that you behold, and that is his true appearance. He has barely aged despite his advanced years. Perhaps this is why your other efforts to locate him have been unsuccessful. Your agents were seeking an ancient wizard, not such a young man."

"Your puppet speaks the truth," Archimagus stated flatly. "If you do not believe him, simply remove these chains and I will show you beyond question who I am."

Haeron stared into Archie's eyes and was startled by the power she saw glaring back at her. "That will not be necessary," she said in a much more even tone. "I can see the truth now. Amazing. A trick of such magnitude is worthy of no less a greatness than my own. Who knows, under different circumstances we could have been friends, maybe even more." She caressed his chin with a long bony hand. "Perhaps that could still happen."

"I would sooner die, witch."

"That too can be arranged," she answered, snapping her fingers. "Guards, bring him to my royal torture chamber. The boy too."

At their queen's command, two of her elite bodyguards stepped forward and roughly dragged the prisoners off their horses.

"It seems you have done well after all," Haeron told the still groveling Yens. "You have earned your reward."

"Thank you, my liege," Yens responded with humility. "May I ask another boon of you? It would mean a great deal to me if you were to allow me to witness their torture and execution."

Haeron stared forcefully at Yens, and the man winced involuntarily at her piercing red eyes. "I don't usually grant favors," she finally said, "but for the conqueror of Archimagus I will make an exception. Come with me."

*   *   *

"It's starting!"

Aimee raised her right hand and examined it. At first she didn't see anything, but then she noticed a faint outline. Gillian was right. The magic was wearing off and they were becoming visible.

"You look like a ghost," Gillian told her.

"You too," Aimee answered with a giggle. "I can see right through you. What do we do now?"

"Now we have to tread as carefully as possible, sister. If we can see each other then others will be able to see us as well. Do you have the map?"

Aimee relaxed her left hand and released the grip she had on Gillian's. Now that they were able to see each other they didn't need to hold hands to keep from losing each other. Reaching past the ball that she was still clinging on to, she pulled a piece of paper out of her pocket. She wrinkled her nose as she unfolded the map with a frown. "I have it right here, but I can't read it yet. When Archie made us invisible he made our clothes invisible too. I guess because this was in my pocket it was also affected. We'll have to wait until the spell wears off better before I can read it."

Gillian nodded her semi-transparent head. She was a warrior, eager for the battle to begin. Still, as she once reminded Aimee, the teachings of Airia described patience as a virtue. They would wait.

* * *

"Perhaps I was foolish to take prophesy so seriously, my lord governor."

Yens swallowed hard. Saying the right thing now would keep him in Haeron's good graces. The wrong words could get him knocked to the floor again. Or worse. Here in her private torture chamber anything could happen. Dozens of implements of pain and torture decorated the large room, and pools of dried blood stained the stone floor beneath nearly every one. "How so, Mistress?"

"Have you ever heard of Natrix?"

"Natrix the prophet?"

"Natrix the false prophet. She predicted that Archimagus would be reunited with the resurrected Fortis and together they would dethrone me before Midsummer's feast. Said she saw it in the stars. I put her to death for such heresy, but I must confess that her words did worry me. That is why I insisted that you deliver the magician to me before tomorrow's feast."

Haeron glided across the room and cradled Archie's chin in her hand again. With a soft, soothing motion she caressed his cheek gently. Then, striking as abruptly as a snake, she dug her nails into his skin and raked them down the side of his face. A trail of blood was left in their wake. "If this is the mighty Archimagus, it appears I had nothing to fear."

* * *

"I think they're gone," Gillian said as the footsteps faded into silence.

Aimee peeked carefully around the corner. The corridor was completely empty. "Come on."

They walked slowly, Aimee reading her map and looking for landmarks as Gillian used her warrior skills to keep them from being sighted. The command panel that controlled the operation of the drawbridge was deep in the heard of the castle. Their quest had been interrupted several times already by roaming patrols.

They came to an intersection of hallways, and Aimee paused to get her bearing while Gillian carefully checked each direction for guards.

"This way, I think," Aimee said, pointing down the passage to the right. The corridor was completely deserted and they were able to make up for some of their lost time. Twice more they had to stop and hide from passing patrols, but it wasn't long before they reached their destination.

"According to the map this should be it," Aimee said as they stopped before one final intersection.

"Which way?"

"Left."

Gillian checked to make sure that they were still alone before the girls stepped into the opening. They turned, expecting to see the controls but what they found instead was a railing.

"I don't get it," Aimee whispered. The disappointment and fear were evident in her voice. "The map says the control panel should be right here."

"There doesn't seem to be anything here at all, sister."

"I know," Aimee acknowledged. "We're on some kind of balcony." Creeping on all fours she approached the railing and looked over. "Come here, Gillian. I think I've found the problem. We're up one floor too many."

Gillian crawled to the railing and poked her head over carefully. Sure enough, there on the floor below was the lever that opened and closed the drawbridge. There were no guards in sight and the girls felt safe enough to stand up.

Gillian looked straight down. "It's too far to jump," she said with certainty. Is there another way down?

"Not nearby," Aimee answered after consulting the map. "The only staircase I can see is way back where we first started. There's no way we can make it there and back before the sun goes down."

"Then we've failed."

"Maybe not," Aimee responded. She pulled the ball out of her jacket pocket and looked at it. "I've been carrying this around since we first came to Daak. Maybe I can put it to good use."

"How?"

"A couple of weeks ago, in what seems like another lifetime, Rodney and I snuck into a neighbor's yard and picked some apples we weren't supposed to. We both tried to hit a pumpkin with them. I missed, and Rodney made fun of me for throwing like a girl." Aimee took another look at the ball in her hand. Pulling it back, she glared at the lever with determination. "I'll show him what a girl can do."

Aimee mouthed a silent prayer as she studied the angle of the throw. Taking careful aim, she snapped her arm forward, releasing the ball as hard as she could. It whistled through the air before hitting the lever with a thud. Just as she hoped it would, the force of the impact jarred the lever, moving it.

For a moment it seemed like nothing was happening. Then, suddenly, a loud rattling filled the air as the chains moved to let the drawbridge down. Just as suddenly, two figures appeared below. They were guards running to pull the lever back up and raise the bridge.

Without hesitation, Gillian hopped onto the railing of the balcony and launched herself into the air. She timed her flight perfectly and came down on top of one of the guards, using his body to break her fall. A punch, a kick, and he was out. She turned to engage the other one. The second guard, a hulk of a man, laughed, amused at such a tiny opponent. He was so confident, in fact, that he threw his only weapon, a large double-bladed sword, to the ground. That was a fatal mistake.

Gillian dove forward, grabbing the larger man by the ankle. With one powerful twist, she managed to knock him off his feet. As he struggled to stand back up, she leapt to her feet and ran for the sword that he had so carelessly tossed aside. Back on his feet now, the guard spun to find Gillian. He turned just in time to see her, sword in hand, thrusting the weapon in his direction. It was the last thing that he would ever see. As the guard dropped, sword embedded in his chest, Gillian casually bent down and scooped Aimee's ball off the floor.

"That's it," Aimee shouted down from above. "The drawbridge is down and we've done our part in the plan. Now all we have to do is wait."

Gillian pulled her arm back and threw the ball back to her friend. "How can we just wait when the most glorious events are yet to unfold, sister? Come, there is a battle to join."

* * *

“Mistress,” Galen shouted as he threw the door to the torture room open. Sweat was dripping from his face and he was out of breath.

Haeron glowered at the intrusion. “This had better be important, cockroach. The night is young. If you’ve interrupted me for nothing, I’ll have plenty of time to work on you after I put these two to death.”

Galen swallowed hard. He knew he was risking his queen’s wrath by bursting in like this, but he had no other choice. To not tell her now would mean certain death when she found out later. “A million pardons, but the fortress is under attack.”

“What? How is this possible?”

“Somehow, the drawbridge was lowered without authorization and the Wards swarmed in. Even as we speak they are engaging our forces in battle.”

“So?” Haeron shrugged her shoulders, a cackling laugh working its way from deep within her chest. “How much of a fight can a bunch of idiotic Wards put up? This should be the shortest battle in the history of Daak.”

“That’s what our soldiers thought at first, too, but the Wards are pushing our troops deeper into the castle. Already they’ve killed or captured nearly half your guards. Hand to hand combat isn’t working, and it’s starting to look like the only way we’ll be able to beat them back is if you use your magic. They fight like Truculans.”

“That’s because they are Truculans,” Yens said smugly.

“What? Explain yourself, lord governor.”

“There is little to explain, your highness,” Yens said, taking a deep bow. When he straightened back up he was clutching his staff firmly in both hands. “The descendants of the Truculans haven’t been holed up in the icy wasteland of Frieer. They’ve been hiding right in front of you all these years posing as the stupid Wards and waiting for the right time to reclaim the planet. Now is the time.” He pointed his staff at Archie and Rodney. “Natrix was hardly a false prophet, sorceress. Her predictions will come true tonight, for Archimagus and Fortis have indeed been reunited. And you, Haeron, through your plan to capture Archimagus, are the one who brought them together.”

Haeron lifted her arm and pointed an open hand at Yens. “Traitorous bug! Prepare to die!” A ball of blue energy formed and crackled with intensity at her fingertips. With a flip of her wrist the ball went flying toward Yens, sizzling as it sliced through the air.

Yens flinched instinctively, but there was really no reason to do so. The globe of energy splattered against an invisible barrier and dissipated harmlessly into the air long before it could hit him.

"Who dares?" the evil sorceress demanded, but she already knew the answer. There was only one man on the planet with that kind of power. Across the room Archimagus stood tall, the magical handcuffs dangling open in his hands.

"Quickly, Galen," Haeron ordered. "Summon my elite guard."

Her chief advisor bolted out the door at her command.

"Stop him," Archimagus ordered, pointing at the fleeing man. "This fight must be just between us."

With a nod of understanding, Yens tightened the grip on his staff and chased after Galen.

"You know you cannot beat me," Haeron snapped as she turned to face Archimagus. "Passive white magic can never defeat black magic."

"We shall see, witch. Give it your best shot."

Not one, but two orbs of glowing energy flickered into being and churned in her fingertips this time. One in each hand. She flung them at Archie and he was able to shrug them off with a wave of his own hand.

"If that's the best you can do, this will be a short battle indeed."

"Mock me not, mage," Haeron sneered. Clasping her hands together, she summoned a much larger ball of energy, at least as big as her head, and whipped it at Archie. He stumbled slightly under the impact, but managed to maintain his footing. Standing straight, he prepared for her next attack.

Archie bent his knees slightly waiting for the next energy ball to hit his magical shield, but it didn't come. Instead, the horrible sorceress chose another target and sent the deadly energy careening in Rodney's direction. Archie acted quickly, throwing his shield over the boy to stop the onslaught of energy. He wasn't able to bring his shield back to himself quickly enough, however, and the next bolt hit him straight on and punched him into the wall. Like a teddy bear that had lost its stuffing, he fell limply to the ground. A pool of blood was forming at the corner of his mouth, and one of his arms was twisted so far behind his back that it had to be broken.

"You were right," Haeron laughed as she stared at Archie's crumpled form with approval. "This was a short battle. So much for prophesy, slug. Prepare to die."

Archie forced a weak smile to his lips as he watched the evil sorceress grow another energy ball in her fingertips. Struggling, he raised his one good arm above his head and took a deep breath. **"Demacle! Viticle! Rapathie!"**

Haeron sneered. Swearing under her breath, she threw the ball of energy as hard as she could. It arced through the air, sending sparks flying in every direction. The ball hit Archie square in the chest, exploding with such intensity that Haeron and Rodney were both forced to cover their eyes.

"What treachery is this?" she screamed as the smoke cleared to reveal the damage. She was staring at the point where her energy ball had exploded, but there was no body! Archimagus was gone!

Haeron spun and searched the room, but the magician was nowhere to be seen. "If you think a spell of invisibility will save you, Truculan, you are fatally mistaken," she shouted at the air around her. Concentrating, she whispered a spell in the tongue of the ancients. Almost immediately, a dark blue mist filled the air. Swirling, it dropped down from the ceiling clinging to everything it came into contact with. The torture equipment, Rodney, even Haeron herself became covered with this blue glow but there was still no sign of Archimagus. Furious, Haeron whipped her arm in circles above her head and the blue mist disappeared from everything. She turned and glared at Rodney.

"I don't know how your friend escaped me, but I still have you."

"Correction," Rodney said with Archie's voice. "You still have us both, or rather we still have you. I believe we have some unfinished business."

The sorceress was incredulous. Archie was hiding in the one place she would have never thought to look for him. Inside Rodney. "This trick doesn't impress me," she lied. "It just makes my job easier. Now I'll be able to kill you both with one blow." With a flick of her wrist she sent another energy ball screaming through the air.

Archie had regained his strength through Rodney. No. He had more than regained it. He had increased it by at least three-fold. Archie/Rodney didn't bother with a shield this time. He/they simply swatted the ball away as easily as a horse might swat a fly with its tail. Haeron sent more bolts flying, but Archie/Rodney batted those away just as effortlessly.

Haeron backed off as Archie/Rodney moved in her direction. She continued to throw the balls, and they continued to be knocked away. Finally, the dark sorceress found herself backed up against the wall. Trapped between two of her own torture devices, she summoned up all her strength and formed one giant energy orb so big that she stumbled under its weight as she clutched it with both hands. Heaving it like a medicine ball, she threw it at Archie/Rodney.

Instead of slapping this one away, Archie/Rodney caught it. It was so big and so powerful that it sent he/them staggering, but he/they managed to catch his/their balance and with great effort send the ball flying back toward the dark sorceress.

Haeron held her hands in front of her face but they offered little protection. Her own weapon was coming back at her and there was nothing she could do to stop it. She screamed as the energy impacted, the explosion throwing her body into the air. She hit the hard cement of the wall with a thud and slithered to the ground unconscious.

Archie/Rodney lifted his/their hands into the air. **"Elcamed! Lcitiv! Eihtapar!"**

A clap of thunder echoed through the chamber, and when its sound died away Rodney and Archie were standing side-by-side as two separate beings again. Both were breathless from the ordeal, and Archie's right arm was hanging limply at his side, still broken from where Haeron's energy had pounded him against the wall before the merger.

Rodney inched over to the evil sorceress and nudged her with his toe. Nothing. "Is she dead?"

Archimagus bent down and examined her with his good hand. "I don't know how she survived that onslaught of energy, but no. She's still very much alive."

"What happens now?"

Haeron's hands whisked up like bullets and grabbed Archie by the throat. "Now you both die, starting with your magician friend. That was a clever trick, uniting bodies like that to combine your strengths, and you probably would have beaten me if you hadn't given up as soon as I went down. My bet is that you don't have the power left to pull that trick off again. I have won."

"Do something, Archie," Rodney pleaded. "Don't let it end like this. Make us become one again."

"The witch is right," Archie answered, straining to speak through Haeron's vice-like grip around his throat. "I can't." He feebly struggled with his one good arm to break the hold she had on his neck, but he just didn't have the strength left. Archie wheezed, trying to pull air into his lungs, but the sorceress continued to squeeze, closing off his windpipe.

Haeron stared at Rodney. "Sit back and enjoy the show," she cackled. "As soon as your friend is dead, you'll be next."

"No," Rodney cried. He lunged at her, hoping that somehow he could help Archie pull free but then stopped suddenly. Turning, he bolted in the opposite direction.

"Run all you want," Haeron shouted after him. "You won't get far before my guards recapture you. In the meantime, with the death of Archimagus, my rule over Daak will be ensured forever."

Rodney ran, but not far. As he had hoped, Haeron was so caught up with her lust for blood and death that she was focusing on the struggling Archimagus and ignoring everything else. As Archie's body started to go limp in the witch's hands, Rodney bent down and scooped the magical handcuffs off the floor, cradling them so they didn't rattle. Circling around, he snuck up behind the sorceress. Her hands were still clamped around Archie's throat so that they were less than a foot apart. Perfect. With one fluid motion he swung the cuffs around, locking one end onto each of her bony wrists. She dropped Archie in surprise.

"You will die first for that," Haeron barked. She held her handcuffed arms out, her palms facing the ceiling, and summoned another one of her energy balls. Nothing happened. Not even a sparkle.

"Good thinking, Rodney," Archie coughed as he sucked air into his lungs. With a great deal of effort he pulled himself to his feet. "Another few seconds and I would have been dead."

"Curse you both," the Sorceress hissed when she realized what had happened. I will have my revenge."

Rodney took a good look at the woman who had enslaved millions and almost killed both him and Archie. He wanted to hate her, but all he could do was feel pity. "What will happen to her now?"

"I don't think that's for either of us to decide," Archie answered. "The people will hold court as it should be, and their decision will be final. But come, there is one last thing that must be done."

* * *

To say the battle went well would be an understatement. Surprise was on their side, and the Wards had Haeron's guards on the defensive right from the beginning. When word came down through the ranks that the Wards were, in actuality, the descendants of the Truculans, the queen's soldiers became nervous. When their pleas for help from their dark mistress went unanswered the soldiers became downright afraid, and when rumors that Haeron had been defeated started to spread, most of the soldiers surrendered. The Wards combed the castle for any last pockets of resistance, and soon the castle was secure.

They gathered in the courtyard, the prisoners roped off in the center with the Wards, Yens and the girls roaming aimlessly waiting for confirmation that the war had been won. They didn't have to wait for long.

Archimagus and Rodney appeared on one of the battlements overlooking the courtyard. Between them, the handcuffed sorceress looked down at the Wards with contempt. "After all these years it's finally over," Archie shouted, lifting his left arm in victory. His right arm was bound to his chest with a hastily-made sling. "Haeron is defeated and Daak belongs to its people once again. Even now, news of our victory is spreading across the planet and Haeron's forces are surrendering by the thousands. We have won."

A loud battery of cheers rang up from the courtyard below, and Archie had to wait before continuing. "My friends," he said when it was quiet enough again, "I would now like to do something we've all been waiting a long time for." Holding his left arm out, he pointed it palm up towards the crowd. He spoke the words of the ancients, and a bright, almost blinding light bathed the courtyard. When it subsided there wasn't a single Ward left in the area. In their places stood the descendants of the Truculans in their natural forms. Some were tall, some were short. Some were fat and some were skinny. Some were dark-skinned and some were light-skinned. Some were women and some were men, but they were all themselves again for the first time in centuries. A second round of cheers lifted from the courtyard and this time Archie didn't wait for it to die down. He wanted to go join the celebration.

CHAPTER TWENTY-ONE
The Greatest Spell of All

The Midsummer's Feast was held exactly as Haeron had planned. Well, maybe not exactly as planned. Haeron wasn't there. She spent the feast in her dungeon, her magic held in check by her own handcuffs. Word spread quickly of her capture, and most civilized nations of Daak sent emissaries to sit on her trial. Many called for her death, but in the end mercy won out and the people decided that she would remain a prisoner of the Truculans, handcuffed until Archimagus could figure out a way to remove her powers permanently. Yens took it upon himself to oversee the preparations for the feast personally. He had, after all, made a promise to Rodney that he was determined to keep. Thousands attended the celebration eager to express their thanks to the liberators of Daak.

Rodney enjoyed the party, eating to his heart's content. At first he was embarrassed by all the attention he was receiving, but he quickly grew to like it. He was getting used to the word 'hero' and didn't mind it anymore when people called him Fortis. Aimee and Gillian, on the other hand, were far more reserved. They mingled among the crowd, talking to individual persons but trying to stay out of the limelight as much as possible. Still, they had as good a time as Rodney and it was well after midnight before the party broke up and everyone retired for the night.

The next morning, they all gathered together for breakfast. Aimee sat silently and didn't touch a thing. Despite all that they had eaten the evening before, Yens and Rodney shoveled mouthful after mouthful of eggs and sausage and pancakes and bacon into their mouths. It reminded Aimee of the very first breakfast Yens served on Daak.

"Is something wrong, sister?" Gillian asked.

"Kind of," Aimee admitted. "I think it's about time that Rodney and I leave. Our parents are probably worried sick over where we've been. I'll bet our faces are on every milk carton in every store back home."

"What does that mean?"

"Nothing. It just means that it's time for us to go home."

Gillian lowered her head. "Do you think that I can go with you to your home? My sisters will never take me back to mine, and there is nothing else for me here."

"I wouldn't say there's nothing for you here," Archie interrupted. "It will be a difficult job resurrecting the Truculan Empire and restoring order to Daak. Haeron may be defeated, but other evil persons are hurrying to fill the gap that she left. It will be years before the Truculans have overthrown all of her regional governors and restored peace everywhere. We will need every warrior we have to succeed. You have proved yourself to be a valuable asset to our cause. Don't abandon us now."

"I don't know," Gillian said, speaking in a less than serious tone. "Me, a sister of Airia, working with all these men."

"Actually, we were thinking of you commanding many of these men. My people may be descendants of the original Truculans, but there is still a lot that you can teach them. What do you say, General Gillian?"

"General Gillian," she repeated, her chest swelling with pride. "I like the way that sounds. But what about Yens?"

"Yes," Rodney echoed. "What about Yens?"

"This battle could not have been won without Yenspetsnicksnack's assistance," Archie answered as he put a hand on the other man's shoulder. "It was a brave and dangerous thing that he did, denouncing his past and standing up for what he knew was right. He demonstrated the qualities of a true Truculan and there will be a high place for him in the new order. But enough about that. Your sister is right. It's time for you to go."

The twins stood up and hugged Yens and Gillian in turn. With a tear, they turned to face Archie.

"Are you ready?"

"Yes."

"Then get ready for the greatest spell of all." Archie quickly embraced them both and then, without another word, he lifted his left arm (his right was now in a splint) and passed it over the heads of the twins.

Aimee shivered, and Rodney held on to her hand for support. Daak was fading away, and Rodney's bedroom at home was beginning to take its place. "Will we ever meet again?" Rodney shouted at the disappearing forms.

"We already have," Archie's voice answered mysteriously, but there was no body to go with it. They were now completely back in Rodney's room and only time would tell what Archie meant by that.

"This is it," Aimee let go of her brother's hand. "Home at last."

"I know," he nodded, not knowing whether to be happy or sad about it. There was no time to decide. Their parents had heard the noise of their return and came rushing into the room.

"You're back," Father sobbed, wiping back a tear. He grabbed both of them and wrapped his arms tightly around them. "Thank God you're back."

"Your father and I have been so worried," Mother added, running over and joining the hug. There were questions to ask, but now was not the time for words. She squeezed harder and let her tears flow freely.

And while the family delighted in being together again, a single drawing sat unnoticed on Rodney's table. Everyone in it was smiling.

Coming Soon

QUEEN AIMEE THE WISE

Book Two of the Daak Trilogy

Printed in the United States
3394

9 781591 130680